PRAISE FOR THE NOVELS OF STEPHANIE HANSEN

"This was a wild ride from start to finish! The concept was super intriguing, and the pacing kept things moving in the best way. The characters had great chemistry, and the story blended action and emotion really well. It totally gave off "just one more chapter" energy. Definitely a strong start to something epic."

Crossroad Reviews ~, Bookseller

"With just the right mixture of science fiction and action/adventure, I love the unexpected twists and mysteries that the characters encounter. The way that the multiple dystopian worlds come together on their adventures is unpredictable, and it is all wrapped up with an unforeseen yet satisfying conclusion."

Reviewed By Amy Powers for Readers' Favorite

"The best part of the book is the romance between Austria and Josh, and the ending. And the parts having to do with the lives of the street kids."

Carol Cartaino, former Editor-in-Chief, Writer's Digest Books

"I'm always happy when Irish folklore is added to a story, we don't see enough of the Irish myths and legends in books. I thought Molly and Orla were interesting and unique characters and enjoyed getting to know them and the rest of the cast. I was invested in the plot and thought it was a good way of a potential series."

Kathryn M, NetGalley Reviewer

GUARDED TIME

Stephanie Hansen

HYPOTHESIS
productions

The text type was set in Castellar, Harlow, and Times New Roman. Cover design by Fay Lane. Interior artwork by @flandivel. Editing by Tru Story and Readers Together.

ALSO BY STEPHANIE HANSEN

Altered Helix

Stranded Coil

Paralleled Bond

Replaced Parts

Omitted Pieces

Ghostly Howls

Armored Hours

SUGGESTED READING ORDER

Altered Helix (Altered Helix 1)

Stranded Coil (Altered Helix 2)

Paralleled Bond (Altered Helix 3)

Replaced Parts (Transformed Nexus 1)

Omitted Pieces (Transformed Nexus 2)

Ghostly Howls (Ghostly 1)

Armored Hours (Reincarnation Spells 1)

Guarded Time (Reincarnation Spells 2)

Ghostly Returns (Ghostly 2) – not yet released

For those who love someone fighting addiction—you are loved, you are seen.

GUARDED

TIME

Stephanie Hansen

BREACH

Cromwell taking Drogheda by Storm

Drogheda was known for its impenetrable defenses, but Cromwell had a plan. He brought in powerful siege artillery and relentlessly bombarded the town walls. After an ultimatum was rejected, troops stormed the town and slaughtered any resistance. Even civilians were not spared. This event is still considered an awful stain on Cromwell's reputation today. It took place on September 11, 1649.

CHAPTER ONE – CLAUDIA

"IT IS IN EACH OTHER'S SHADOW
THAT PEOPLE LIVE.
A LIGHT HEART LIVES LONG.
OUT WITH THE BADNESS
AND IN WITH THE GOODNESS."

IRISH WITCHCRAFT EVERYDAY
IRISH PAGAN SCHOOL

As the final words of the time travel spell leave my lips, I turn to our friends and bid them farewell with a heartfelt, "Until we meet again, Awen."

Mother, Alex, and I disappear in a flash, surrounded by swirling scenes from our world. My senses are overwhelmed as I struggle to comprehend what is happening.

A powerful hum resonates between us, reverberating the last word spoken by our friends. The pungent aroma of burnt oak leaves fills my nostrils, and smoke curls above us before seeping into my lungs. I can only assume that Alex and Mother are experiencing the same sensations, but it's hard to tell as my body twists and turns.

Suddenly, I feel warmth envelop my hand as Alex grasps it tightly. It grounds me and brings a sense of completeness and contentment. My spirit calms down for a moment, but then our bodies collide as we land in an unknown location. As our eyes meet, a rush of heat spreads through my chest.

I realize we have landed in some kind of cave or underground chamber. Light streams in through small openings in the stone above us. Alex shifts beneath me, likely discomforted by the hard cave floor.

"Where are we?" he croaks.

"I think it's a cave."

"When are we?" he asks hesitantly.

"Hopefully 1649," I reply, my nerves heightening.

"It smells like minerals," Alex observes after taking a deep breath.

"And it's damp," I add. "Definitely a cave, but why are we here?"

"Wait, do you feel that draft?" Alex asks excitedly.

I lean back to allow room for him to move and get onto my knees. A tingling sensation runs under my skin where we were touching moments ago.

"Claudia!" Mother's voice echoes from somewhere within the cave.

"It's Marie," Alex exclaims. "But I can't pinpoint her location because of all the echoes."

"Welcome to my world," I quip back while smiling at him, referring to how my unilateral deafness makes it impossible for me to determine the direction of noise.

"She sounds far away. How will we find her?" Alex asks, concern in his voice.

As I stand up from our resting spot in the small alcove, I become acutely aware of how little light reflects off the thick, stone walls. One wrong step and someone could easily trip and fall.

"Perhaps it's just the location," I suggest, making my way to one side while trying not to lose my balance. "We're here," I add, calling out to Mother.

"Or maybe the walls are so thick that sound is distorted." Alex carefully navigates his way toward a wall without stumbling.

"Claudia? Alex?" Mother's voice echoes throughout the cavern. She must be searching for us too.

Suddenly, a flicker of firelight illuminates an opening in the wall. "Mother, where did you find that torch?" I ask in surprise.

"I lived here in a past life," she reminds us as she pulls out a leather journal from her bag. "My sister and I often met in this cave when we were young. My name was Mary back then."

"Well, now that you've found us, can you lead us out of here?" Alex asks with a hint of impatience.

"Not just yet." Mother takes a seat near Alex and places the torch in a holder. "We still have some things to discuss before we venture out into this world," she explains.

Alex barely restrains a huff but takes a seat next to her, nonetheless. I join them, relieved to see they're at least civil with each other now. It's amazing how far they've come since their rocky first meeting. I know that if it wasn't for Alex's help in finding me and the counters, Mother may have never accepted him. Before all of this, she had been determined to find me a suitable husband from the most eligible bachelors in town—certainly not a bootlegger like Alex.

"I remember bits and pieces of this past life," I say as Mother flips through her journal, "but my memories from future timelines are much clearer."

"That could mean you were right," Mother muses. "We needed to come back to where it all began, but the creator of the counters and dual timelines knew this too. There's definitely something interfering with our plans."

"Which is why we need to be prepared," Alex interjects, bringing us back to the task at hand.

As Mother continues to skim through her journal from the past, I share any memories that come to mind.

"In my memories, I can recall vast green fields, rocky cliffs, and endless blue skies," I say.

"I look forward to seeing that," Alex responds, excitement filling his voice.

"And now, we can finally speak more freely about magic," Mother adds with a smile. "We have nothing holding us back anymore."

"Truly?" I ask, leaning closer to hear her words clearly.

"Yes, in this time and in our home country, the belief in faeries was strong. The people would often use salt to ward off evil spirits," Mother explains, a mischievous grin spreading across her lips.

I nod, understanding the significance of salt as a protective element.

"I believe the tradition of using salt will continue in the future for many people, while the idea of faeries may only remain a childhood fantasy," I respond.

Alex perks up at the mention of faeries. "Do you mean the little beings with wings?"

I smile at his curiosity and whimsy. "Well, yes, those are usually the ones believed to bring magic and help people live longer."

Alex and I exchange a knowing glance. I can't help but wonder what would have happened if my mother had tried reaching out to the faeries to save my aunt Elizabeth from her fate instead of reincarnation, but then I wouldn't have met Alex.

Mother continues, "The Aos Sí, our version of faeries, often appear in the form of hares instead of small, winged creatures like in traditional faerytales."

"What else should we expect in this time period?" I ask, already feeling a bit overwhelmed at all of the differences between my timeline and this one.

"We will need to acquire new clothing. Luckily, Elizabeth and I kept some here for emergencies. We can borrow them."

Alex and I share a look of amazement. It seems she was well-prepared for this journey, almost as if she foresaw it coming.

"The food may take some getting used to, though," Mother warns us.

"I would eat just about anything right now," Alex interjects with a laugh. "I'm starving."

Mother reaches into her bag and pulls out a tin filled with sandwiches wrapped in wax parchment. She hands us each one, and we eagerly devour them. It's only then that I realize how hungry I truly am.

"In this time period, you'll likely be eating things like lamb stew, fadge or potato bread instead of modern meals like peanut butter and jelly sandwiches or reubens," Mother informs us as we eat.

I reach for Alex's hand, feeling both excited and nervous about this new experience.

"We'll also need to learn some basic Irish, as that is the language commonly spoken here," Mother adds.

Alex's eyes widen at the thought of having to learn a new language.

"Not to change the subject, but I'm remembering something else—an impressive structure in town. It was two towers connected by a bridge," I offer, trying to ease his tension.

Alex's features soften, his eyes taking on a glimmer of hope. "That sounds intriguing."

"Ah, that is Laurence's Gate. It's a barbican built as part of the walled fortification of this town, Drogheda."

"I remember the beautiful arch entrance and thinking it looked like a castle."

"Yes, it still survives in the 1920 timeline we traveled from. Cromwell's artillery bombardment that breached the walls could not bring down the gate."

The mention of the attack brings a sorrowful look to Mother's face, one I can't bear to see. "How about the Irish we're meant to learn?"

Watching Alex listen intently is endearing. As he picks up where we left off with the language lesson, memories flood back to me with newfound clarity. Though I was born after the siege, I had heard stories about it my entire life during this 17th century timeline. It's hard to believe that I'm now standing here on the brink of it.

Voices echo through the cave, interrupting our lesson.

"Be quiet," Mother urges. She points to an alcove I hadn't noticed before. As Alex and I move toward it, she gathers her belongings—sandwich wraps, tin, and her diary—into her bag. Once she joins us in the alcove and extinguishes the torch, we're enveloped in almost complete darkness. The voices grow louder.

"That's me from the past," Mother whispers anxiously. "I cannot see myself. It could disrupt the future entirely."

"We'll remain silent," Alex whispers reassuringly.

"So, Elizebeth, Aunt Anna's past soul, is here with you then?" I ask quietly.

"Yes," Mother confirms.

We hold our breath and stay as still as possible. The footsteps draw closer until they are audible, but it's impossible to determine their direction. And then, they come into view, their torchlight casting flickering shadows across the walls of the cave. We huddle closer together behind cover to remain hidden.

"Níl a fhios agam cá bhféadfadh sé a bheith," one of them says in a familiar voice—Mother's, but not the one standing next to me. It's my mother from the past, Mary instead of Marie.

I glance over at my mother and see her reach for the torch. Whatever was said must have caught her attention. Did they notice it was missing? I hope they don't come looking for it.

"Tabharfaidh mé ceann eile liom an chéad uair eile. Aimseoigh muid é."

Even though it's a voice I've never heard before, I would recognize that soul anywhere, Anna! My mother brings a delicate hand to her mouth, holding back a gasp. A single tear glistens down her cheek, reflecting the faint light of their torch.

I can't help but react similarly. Memories of Anna flood my mind. The woman who had watched over my friends before ever meeting them. A pillar in the vibrant community of Kansas City in 1920. And here she is, alive and well in 1649. She had given her life to save mine.

Hearing her speak again, even in this timeline where she is much younger, stirs up a whirlwind of emotions within me. Warmth mixed with the sharp pain of loss.

"Ar scáth a chéile a mhaireann na daoine," they both say in unison.

My mother joins in their chant as if it were out of her control. Thankfully, she whispers, but I still try to muffle the sound by softly placing my hand over her mouth.

"Maireann croí éadrom i bhfad." A gentle breeze swirls around us, carrying the cool dampness with it.

Elizabeth and Mary carefully lift bundles of fragrant lavender out of a nearby basket, followed by a coil of rope. More memories flood in: Alex finding us when our ship had vanished into thin air.

"An donas amach is an sonas isteach." I can tell we are witnessing some of my mother's first magical abilities. It is both awe-inspiring and heart-wrenching to witness. I am grateful for the woman who has raised me through countless timelines.

Despite all the heartbreak we have endured and the overwhelming odds we now face, seeing these two powerful women gives me a glimmer of hope.

All too soon, their magic training session comes to an end, and they pack up their belongings.

Once they have left and we have waited the same amount of time it took for them to enter, we carefully exit the small alcove.

"It's getting late," my mother says to us. "I know where some extra blankets are kept." And with that, she is off to retrieve them.

"How are you holding up?" Alex asks, placing his comforting hands on my arms. All I can do is lean into him and let out a deep sigh. He embraces me in a warm hug, as if he could read my thoughts perfectly.

With a soft rustle of blankets and the flickering light of an additional torch, Mother returns to our makeshift campsite. Her face is tired and drawn from the time travel journey we've been on. She gestures toward an additional alcove that I had somehow missed before. "I'll sleep over there," she announces quietly before setting up her bed without another word.

Alex and I follow suit, arranging our own sleeping area and settling in for the night. Mother's gentle snores are soon heard, lulling us into a sense of safety and comfort amidst the unfamiliar surroundings. As Alex wraps his arm around me, I turn to face him.

"We can solidify our plans tomorrow," he whispers, brushing a stray strand of hair behind my ear. The warmth of his touch spreads throughout my body, igniting a fire inside me.

Our lips meet in a slow and tender kiss, but it quickly builds into something more passionate. I grip his hair while he gently angles his head for a deeper connection. Our bodies press together, our hearts beating in perfect synchronization.

"Claudia," Alex groans in protest as I push him to the edge.

I know what a respectable girl should not do, but after everything we've been through and traveling hundreds of years into the past, I'm pretty sure that rules no longer apply.

"What about your mother?" he manages to say between kisses.

"I know," I whisper back before peppering his face with kisses. He smiles and pulls me closer. "Goodnight, Alex."

Wrapped in his embrace, I drift off to sleep faster than I ever have before, feeling safe and loved in his arms.

CHAPTER TWO – ALEXANDER

TIE A RIBBON OR PIECE OF COLORED FABRIC
ONTO A HAWTHORN TREE AND MAKE A WISH.
THIS IS A REQUEST FOR THE BLESSING OF THE
GODDESS,
AND THESE OFFERINGS MAY ALSO BE
USED LATER FOR HEALING PURPOSES.

As the first rays of sun peeked through the cracks in the cave walls, I shifted my gaze to Claudia lying next to me. Her delicate features were like those of an angel, radiating a sense of peace and serenity. Meanwhile, my mind was troubled with conflicting visions of the future: a lowly street kid, a struggling fisherman, a survivor of a corrupt facility, and even a bootlegger in my home timeline. But then Claudia's presence would bring warmth and light into every scenario. She stirred awake just then, her bright eyes meeting mine as she smiled and reached up to caress my face. Leaning down, I pressed my lips to hers in a soft kiss, feeling all the unease from my previous thoughts melt away.

"Good morning," I murmured against her lips.

"I'm starving," she replied with a laugh. We shared a smile before pulling each other close.

More sunlight filtered through the openings in the cave, illuminating our little corner. I noticed Marie getting up and stretched out my hand to help Claudia up as well. She ran her fingers through her hair in a familiar and comforting gesture.

"You two are up early," Marie remarked as she walked over to us. "I have some fruit in my bag for breakfast."

We sat down and discussed our plans for the day as we ate the sweet apples. Marie needed a coven for our plans to work, but she couldn't join her own as her soul would recognize itself and trigger unknown consequences. She'd need to find a new one and go under a new name, Laura.

"I remember Róis being a herbalist," Marie said thoughtfully. "She should be at either the tincture shop or her dwelling. I'll stop by the hawthorn tree on the way there."

"Why the hawthorn tree?" Claudia asked curiously.

"Well, it's said to be one of the few gateways to the world of the Fae." A warm grin spread across Marie's face.

Claudia and I exchanged a look of bemusement before she turned to Marie. "You're not planning on leaving us in this world we know nothing about, are you?"

"Of course not, my dear." Marie patted Claudia's leg reassuringly.

"I'll head into town to see if there are any job opportunities," I interjected. "That way, we can ensure our survival and keep an ear out for any threats."

"Please be careful," Claudia begged.

"You're the one who needs to take precaution."

"Why, I'm just going to be with my family," she protested. "Mother has shared the schedule. I know how to make acquaintances."

In order to keep tabs on Elizabeth, old Anna, Claudia would get close to her. Since she had not been born yet, and even Mary, old Marie, had not been aware reincarnation would pass down, we were sure it would work. They'd yet to even meet her soul, so there was no fear of them recognizing her—or so we hoped.

"You'll need to get close enough to be invited to the monthly ritual but not too close," Marie warned.

"Yes, Mother."

"I can't wait to see the vibrant green, towering rock, and endless blue skies you described," I exclaimed, the prospect of seeing sunlight again making me feel more at ease.

"Agreed," Claudia replied. "Let us leave this cave."

Stepping outside, the first thing that struck me was the vivid greenery. It was as if a cloudy day had been transformed into a bright and sunny one, diffusing light and creating a soft glow over everything. The grass was a lush emerald color, making the sky appear more teal than it really was. The water reflected this beauty, giving off an otherworldly feeling. The rocks themselves looked like ancient castle walls, but instead of being built by humans, they were crafted by Mother Nature herself— adding to the overall magnificence of the landscape.

Walking through the trees, I couldn't help but feel they were enchanted. As a hare crossed my path, I thought of Marie's stories of the Fae. The hare sprinted away and then disappeared around a…hawthorn tree. I smiled to myself since Claudia and Marie had taken their own paths.

Emerging from the trees, I could see the impressive Drogheda wall beyond the ripples of grass and water. Laurence's Gate stood tall too. Viewing the buildings that lined the streets, I was reminded just how far in the past we'd traveled. The busy streets were filled with people going about their daily lives—mothers holding their children's hands, horses pulling carts laden with goods, and men leisurely smoking pipes on the sidelines.

A flurry of people rushed past me, all heading in the same direction. As if pulled by a string, I followed along. It wasn't until a group of young lads my age passed by that I began to understand some of the chatter around me. I overheard the word "seanchaithe," which immediately brought to mind Marie's lessons about storytellers. The excitement in the air was palpable. Then, one of the lads mentioned something about news from over the water, likely related to England. I felt reassured in my decision to follow the crowd.

The crowd came to a sudden stop, drawn in by the presence of a man with a hat and cane standing in the center. He spoke with eloquence and passion about his voyage, captivating everyone with his words. His gestures were dramatic, as if his very life had hung in the balance during his travels.

Curiosity piqued within me when I overheard one of the lads next to me mention "airm," which I recognized as weapons or arms. I couldn't resist asking, "Ar luaigh sé airm ó thar an lear?"

Each lad turned to look at me with skeptical gazes. I realized my thick English accent needed some work.

"An spiaire thú?" asked the biggest of the bunch, leaning closer with an intimidating aura.

I shook my head and raised my hands in surrender, or perhaps in protest. "Níl mé, is as na coilíneachtaí Meiriceánacha mé," I replied, grateful for our rehearsed cover story. My nerves were frayed.

"Aren't you going the wrong way?" one of the smaller lads asked in English.

"Yeah, most people are headed to America," chimed in the third lad with a slight laugh. "They arrested my uncle and sent him there. How'd you break out?"

"What are you doing here?" The first man who addressed me still held a stern expression.

"My friend here wants to know which side you're on," added the friendly lad, who had switched to English for my benefit.

"Oh, I hate the Brits," I quickly responded.

The lad with an uncle in America slapped me on the back. "I knew you were one of us. Look at how rough his hands are. No way he's a Sasanach!"

"You didn't know anything," retorted the big man.

"Póg mo thóin!" spat back the lad who had just slapped my back.

Once again, I raised my hands in a gesture of peace and said, "Not a Sasanach—just Alex."

"Deas bualadh leat," said the one who had slapped me. "I'm Liam." He had dark hair and eyes with matching dark circles underneath. As we shook hands, I noticed paint residue spotting his rough skin.

"And I'm Rí," the small and kind lad added with a twinkle in his eye and a warm smile on his face. "Glad to make your acquaintance. Fáilte." His voice was like music, soothing and welcoming, which juxtaposed the face of his daunting friend.

"Conor," the gigantic lad stated simply, his deep voice booming through the air. As he shook my hand with one of the strongest grips I'd encountered, a vision from the future came into focus. In the vision, a man with a similar stature had scared away many solely by his presence, but his actions were completely different, exuding loyalty and serious advocation for those in need.

"We were just heading to the pub as it's our day off," Rí said cheerfully, gesturing toward the quaint stone building behind them. "You're welcome to join us if you'd like."

Conor grunted, his demeanor slightly less friendly than Rí's. Perhaps he was not as kind as the man from my vision after all.

Liam clapped Conor on the back and then turned to me with a grin. "Yeah, we can welcome you to Drogheda with good times and get to know you better."

He and Conor nodded at each other in agreement, as if Liam's choice of words had been perfect.

"Sounds good to me," I replied eagerly.

They led the way down the cobblestone street lined with charming shops and bustling crowds until we reached the pub. The wooden frame around the door and front windows bore the words: Teach Chairbre in bold letters.

As we entered, patrons greeted my new acquaintances warmly and glanced curiously in my direction. I hoped that by becoming closer to these lads, I would gain some acceptance within this new town.

"Go raibh maith agat," Rí said to a woman after she set wooden bowls filled with steaming lamb stew in front of us.

"Leann," Liam called out before she could walk away. Then, he gestured toward our group with a smile.

"Le do thoil," Conor added as he playfully smacked Liam upside the back of his head before turning his attention to his own bowl of stew. Soon enough, we were each brought a silver cup of ale and began to chat.

As we sipped on our drinks and savored the hearty stew, I asked the lads about their occupations. "I'm new to town and looking for employment. What do you all do for work?"

They exchanged curious glances, even Rí seemed taken aback by my question. I quickly realized that I must have made a mistake in my wording.

"You know, job assignments?" I clarified.

"No, no," Conor replied with a chuckle. "Tell us more about yourself first. What kind of work did you do back in America?"

With a thoughtful sip, I pondered my next words carefully. The truth was not an option—there were no bootleggers in America during the 1600s. "I worked in warehouses, moving barrels of booze," I finally replied.

Liam raised his glass and gave me a knowing look. "My kind of man."

Rí jumped into the conversation with excitement. "So you're used to lifting heavy loads? You'd fit right in at the port."

Conor cleared his throat and shot Rí a stern glance that silenced him immediately.

"Is that where you work?" I asked, eager to offer my help, and understanding how they probably became fluent in English. "I don't mind hard labor."

"Lusks don't last long," Conor warned. "It's tough work."

"I'm not afraid to put my nose to the grindstone," I assured them.

As we continued our chat, a group of ladies walked by, and Liam couldn't help but turn his head to watch them go past. He let out a low whistle.

"Well, I don't know about you, but I'm going to talk to one of those beauties," he announced boldly.

I lifted my cup, silently wishing him luck.

"Come with me and see what Ireland has to offer," he urged me.

Shaking my head, I replied, "Sorry, I'm spoken for." Instantly, I regretted it. I was undercover and shouldn't know Claudia yet, but no ounce of me wanted to make a pass, or whatever men did in the 1600s, at the women who just entered. Claudia and I would just have to improvise a new plan.

Conor ended up joining Liam in his pursuit of the ladies while Rí stayed behind with me. Curious, I asked him why he didn't join them.

"I am also spoken for," he replied with a smile.

We ordered more drinks and engaged in deep conversation as we discussed our lives. Rí shared how much he wished his little brother could be there to listen to the seanchaithe. I opened up about my own little brother, who was still back in America, wishing I could tell him more. The truth had to be guarded, though I feared with another round that might be impossible. Liam and Conor had rejoined us and they'd switched to whiskey.

"I should call it a night," I announced, feeling the effects of alcohol starting to take hold.

"But the fun is just getting started!" Liam protested.

"Perhaps it's for the best," Conor interjected. "Report to the dock at sunrise?" He lifted his eyebrows at me.

"See you then," I agreed and nodded in reassurance.

As the candles flickered to life, the room was bathed in a warm glow. But outside, the once sunny streets were now shrouded in darkness, illuminated only by the eerie yellow light of streetlamps. Dread settled in my chest as I realized I may never find my way back to the cave in this unfamiliar time and place.

CHAPTER THREE ~ MARIE

Let's start at the very beginning, a place that held great significance in my life—the hawthorn tree. Its thorny branches twisted and turned, adorned with delicate white flowers that seemed to glow under the warm rays of the sun. Known as crann sceach gheal, this tree held mystical powers that were not to be taken lightly. As the wind rushes through its leaves, gently rustling my hair, I can't help but feel a sense of comfort and grounding in its presence.

This was where my coven would gather to honor Nature and all her blessings. We would bask in the beauty of how each element flowed seamlessly together, from the air filling our lungs to the earth nourishing the roots of the majestic hawthorn before us. In our rituals, we would light a fire at night and circle around it, celebrating the light that fed nature and represented another cycle of life.

As I take a moment to breathe in the memories of those times, I reach into my bag and pull out a silver cup that I had acquired in 1921 in preparation for our time-traveling journey. Filling it with water from the nearby stream, I take a refreshing sip before pouring some at the roots of the hawthorn tree as an offering of praise.

Looking up at the canopy of leaves above me, I am struck by the beautiful sky peeking through. With a purposeful stride, I make my way toward Róis's dwelling to see if she is there.

The scents of nature surround me as I walk, filling my senses with their sweet fragrance. If she is not at her home, then perhaps she will be at her tincture shop.

Climbing over a small hill, I spy her thatched roof first—its distinct smoke hole easily visible. However, no smoke can be seen rising from it today, which likely means Róis is not cooking with her usual modest fire. As I approach the hazel frame of her dwelling, I reach out and touch it.

"Heileo," I call out, knowing that Róis would not recognize me in this form. I must act as a stranger and try to befriend her. The thought makes my stomach flutter nervously, but I remind myself that if I expect Claudia and Alex to successfully infiltrate this world, then surely, I must do the same.

Stepping inside, the first things that catch my eye are the simple furnishings—a bed made of green rush and homespun woolens, a short stool in one corner with a crow feather weighted down by a rock next to it. A flint arrow tip lays nearby, along with a candle whose dried wax drips tell tales of many nights spent in this humble abode. But what I do not see is any sign of a living person here now, which only reinforces my need to continue my search for Róis.

I pick my way carefully along the boggy road, my feet sinking slightly into the damp ground. As I approach the town of Drogheda, memories flood back to me, and it feels like coming home after a lifetime away. The familiar landscape, buildings, and bustling activity make it seem as if time has stood still. I see familiar faces around me, but I keep my emotions in check so as not to give myself away. It would be odd for me to greet them all as old friends now, being in the body of a stranger.

But then I see his face in front of mine, and I can't help but smile. I summon all my strength to remain composed, resisting the urge to run up to him and wrap him in a hug. Gazing upon Barnabus again is like a dream, transporting me back to my first reincarnation stage when I was young and carefree. Our eyes meet, and the warmth between us is palpable. He hesitates, struggling with recognition and conflicting emotions. As someone who has known his soul for ages, I can see it all so clearly.

Clearing my throat, I break eye contact and force myself to move away, feeling a twinge of pain down to my bones. It's crucial that I make it to the tincture shop and find Róis to join her coven as soon as possible. Another encounter like this could be dangerous, no matter how much my heart longs for it. Avoiding any further eye contact, I make a beeline for the shop.

Inside, the tincture shop is a treasure trove of delights. Shelves upon shelves are filled with glass bottles of various sizes and shapes, each containing different herbs, crystals, or flowers. A sense of calm washes over me as I take in the aroma and beauty of it all. On one side of the shop, a table serves as a checkout counter with stacks of books on either side. In the center of the shop, a few small round tables are set up for customers to enjoy tea and read their leaves. A rumor I now know to be true—the tea was stolen off an English ship.

Polite but rusty, I order a cup of tea in Irish. When it arrives, I am delighted by the pretty cup with its smooth surface and shallow bowl. The owner carefully measures out a spoonful of leaves before pouring hot water over them and leaving me to watch the steep in peace. With my cup in hand, I settle into one of the tables and watch as other customers browse the shelves. As I near the bottom of my cup, I think about Róis and feel excitement building inside of me.

With just one small sip left, I stop and swirl the liquid around in my cup three times counterclockwise. Tradition says this is how you see a prophecy. Holding my teacup close to my heart, I focus on my thoughts and feelings. Suddenly, a familiar voice cuts through the air—the very one I've been waiting for. But caution is necessary, as always. Looking down at my tea leaves, I study the patterns and groupings, each one reflecting a different cycle of my many lifetimes. But there's an extra grouping that catches my eye. Could it indicate how our destinies are being manipulated? I can't be sure, but then I see Róis making her way toward the owner's table, and I set down my cup, ready to join her.

With efficient speed, I gather the necessary ingredients: salt, a glass chalice, and a couple of glimmering quartz crystals. As I wait in line behind Róis, I notice she has a bundle of red seaweed moss among her items to purchase. The vibrant hue catches my eye, and I can't help but ask about it.

"An bhfuil casacht ar dhuine?" I inquire about the health benefits of the seaweed.

"Tá go deimhin, agus tá gá agatsa le huisce leighis?" She confirms my diagnosis and inquires about my purchases.

"Faraor, is cosúil gur chaill mé go leor de mo chuid rudaí le linn mo thaisteal," I respond with a hint of regret in my voice.

"And you read leaves?" She raises an elegant eyebrow.

"Is my Irish that bad?" I tease back.

"It's not awful," she responds with a smile. "But it seems like you're a bit out of practice."

"I have been gone awhile," I reply truthfully but still guarded.

"You're not one of those English ladies who have arrived to 'civilize' us, are you?" Róis asks with a mischievous glint in her eye.

"Far from it. If only I had the power to stop them." I sigh.

Her eyebrows raise at my response, and a small smile plays on her lips.

"Would you like some help making your cough remedy?" I offer, changing the subject.

"Sure, you can come to my place," Róis locks her arm in mine. She has always been a warm and welcoming soul. "And while you're there, perhaps you can read my friends' tea leaves as well."

"Beidh sé sin deas," I say with a grin, and it brings a smile to Róis' face. Together, we make our way back to her home as I reminisce about the familiar streets and houses.

My healing water is running a competition against even the advanced medicine of 1920 despite my current location of 1649. So crystal clear, the inverted images make me feel as if I'm living in a mirror world. Like I need anything more confusing than the future and past reincarnation memories running through my head.

Luckily, Róis requests help with her cough remedy, pulling me out of the spiral in which I'd been heading. "How much comfrey did you say?" she asks while leaning over a boiling pot of water.

I walk over to get an estimate of how much water there is. "Just enough to fill the palm of your cupped hand."

She does as I suggest and then adds the same amount of winter heliotrope root.

"Now, cover it and let it simmer while you help me find the perfect place for this water to steep," I say.

A woman walks in holding a small boy in her arms. The boy appears to be about four years old. She takes him to a bed, placing him down delicately. He coughs, turns over, and seems to instantly fall back to sleep.

"Tá an créatúr bocht traochta," she says as she approaches Róis, nodding at the pot.

"Yes, I was able to get red seaweed moss," Róis responds. "Laura's helping me brew it."

The woman's eyes follow to where Róis gestures, me, and says, "Name's Onóra. Thank you."

"Of course," I respond, still recovering from the shock of being called by a new name. "Nice to meet you."

"Where are you from?" she asks.

Another woman enters before I'm able to respond. She wears a colorful shawl, whereas Onóra's is umber. Her dress material seems to be a bit more expensive, but since they were acquaintances in a past life, I know that's only because Onóra simply does not care.

"Cén fáth nár inis tú dom go raibh sé tinn?" she asks Róis.

"I knew you'd be able to sense it and, look, here you are."

All three women hug before the newest arrival approaches the boy and gently places a hand to his forehead. "Do I smell winter heliotrope?"

"Yes, Laura is helping me with a brew for his cough."

It's as if she just notices my presence. "Do I know you?" she asks curiously.

My heart plummets to my stomach. I should have been more careful around Neasa, knowing she's psychic. Of course she'd sense the presence of a traveling soul. Was the name change enough?

"I don't believe so," I reply, hoping my anxiety doesn't burst through my tone.

"You must just have a soul similar or connected to someone I know. I'm Neasa."

I nod and then turn to Róis. "We should be able to strain the liquid to the pot and add the moss now."

Onóra helps Róis while Neasa makes her way to my healing water. "And what's this for?" she asks.

Of course she cuts to the point with the precision of a freshly sharpened knife.

"I just thought healing water would be good to have around with the rumors about a possible attack."

All heads turn toward me, and I wish the faeries would morph me into a hare so I could hop away and hide.

"Haven't I warned you to keep your voices down when discussing those greadadhs within or beyond the gate?" another woman who enters proclaims. Étaín is just as beautiful as I remember—rich, dark, and curly hair paired with a button nose.

"It wasn't us," Róis defends, holding up her hands, throwing me under the wagon. "Laura's new to town and didn't know."

Étaín follows Róis's eyeline and lands on me, assessing me with a gaze many would find intimidating.

"I was just explaining to Neasa why I've made healing water," I proclaim.

"Well, any magic that can keep them out sounds good to me. I'm Étaín."

The boy's dry coughs interrupt the introduction.

"It should be ready now, just need to strain it again," I say as I face Róis.

"Oh, and add some honey," Onóra offers.

"Maybe some apple juice too," Neasa pipes up as she eyes the concoction.

Once complete, Róis walks over to the boy with a jar and spoon. Onóra helps the child sit up and places folded woolens behind his head to prop him. Neasa whispers a request for health to return to the boy while Étaín holds her breath.

Róis fills the spoon, blows on it a bit, and slowly brings it to his mouth. He sips it down and then requests to go back to sleep. As soon as his little back rises and falls in peaceful sleep, the women gather on the other side of Róis' dwelling. Onóra even pulls out a seat for me.

"What do you know about a possible attack?" Étaín inquires like the opening of an interrogation.

"This is my home country even if I haven't been here for some time," I respond.

"That doesn't really answer the question though," Neasa says. "Of course, welcome back, but you've heard about what's going on from far away?"

"Give her some time to answer," Onóra says.

Róis brings us each some tea while giving me a knowing look.

"With the execution of Charles I, I'd heard about rebellion uprisings," I explain. "It was only a matter of time before a brigade was sent. My journey took quite some time to get here. It was upon arrival to Drogheda that I overheard the news of possible attack."

"And which side are you on?" Étaín asks.

"Honestly, I wish we could fully return to the Brehon Law and be done with English common law."

Silence descends upon the group, and then each woman's face fills with a warm smile.

"Wouldn't that be absolutely splendid?" Onóra exclaims.

"It would be liberating and free," Neasa adds. "Like we could breathe again."

"Could you imagine if you dared to defend equal rights to the English?" Étaín asks Neasa.

"Or if you shared your concerns for nature?" She speaks to Onóra.

"If the English government followed your restitution rather than punishment approach to crime?" She turns to Róis.

As each woman warms with Étaín's questions, happiness blossoms inside me.

"I do believe we're in agreement with you about that," Étaín says to me.

"Good," Róis replies, "because now we'll have to trust her, as she's going to read our leaves."

As they gather closer to me, my anxiety decreases. Perhaps it won't be so difficult joining a new coven after all.

Guarded Time

CHAPTER FOUR – CROMWELL

"Drogheda's medieval walls towered up in massive masonry that was almost impregnable. As the second great port after Dublin in that region, its importance was obvious, and it was the guardian of the coastal gateway into Ulster."

The Rebels of Ireland by Edward Rutherfurd (Ballantine, 2007)

"What's going on?" Oliver Cromwell turned on his heel, eyebrows arching in surprise, to find Major Fludd standing behind him. The major—Ruarc—was a man who thrived on structure and order, an irony not lost on Oliver since Ruarc had joined his ranks to disrupt the very sequence of scheduled events he so dearly cherished. True to his nature, Ruarc would adhere to directives even when they clashed with his own beliefs.

"It's easy to take a side when it's the only one you hear," Oliver replied, his voice carrying a weight of unspoken implications.

Ruarc's brow furrowed, confusion creasing his forehead. "We have to follow orders, Sir," he insisted, his tone firm yet questioning.

But blind obedience would spell the end for Oliver's beloved Elizabeth. "All I ask is that we reconvene first," he urged, a desperate plea to buy time. He needed to find a way to change things. He knew Mary was doing the same, but she'd still keep her from him. Mary, Elizabeth's sister, was his fiercest enemy but also, in some respects, his closest friend.

"You called for me," Lieutenant Aodhán Marnell barked as he entered.

The smell of rosewater left Oliver's senses along with the thought of Elizabeth. With Aodhán present, he needed to focus on the new mission. Luckily, his counters' spirits had been able to inhabit his two closest allies in 1649. Without that, his mission would be nearly impossible.

"I call this meeting to order," Oliver said.

"What's going on?" Ruarc repeated himself while all three men sat at the table.

Oliver rolled his eyes in response to the major continuing to use futuristic phrasing. He needed to remind them how proper people spoke in 1649. "Whenever gentlemen take the profession of arms upon them, they ought to study all parts of it from the private to the general."

"Why does it feel like you're speaking in riddles?" Aodhán inquired, his frustration evident.

"Yeah, what do you mean?" Ruarc chimed in, puzzled. "We've already studied this. Or are you referring to something else, like a code of sorts?"

Oliver leaned forward, his gaze intense. "Consider the parts as times instead," he explained. "For there is nothing that will help us more than to be experts of knowledge and diligent in that."

Aodhán, exasperated, ran his hands through his hair, then clasped them behind his head, letting out a deep sigh. "Enough of the proper speak and this stupid code," he demanded. "Are you talking about the time with the altered helixes and the haunted house?"

"We could start there, sure," Oliver conceded, a wry smile touching his lips as he thought, *our story has never been told.* "At that point, we tried to save scientists who could reverse the environmental damage to Earth."

"But we were stopped by that annoying girl, her friends, and family," Ruarc said with a huff, his voice tinged with frustration.

"Or so they thought," Oliver replied, a sly smile playing on his lips, which earned mirrored expressions of cunning from the other two men seated around the dimly lit table.

"So what was the problem with that timeline then?" Aodhán asked, his curiosity piqued.

"Let's not get ahead of ourselves," Oliver cautioned, his tone measured and composed. "I think it's best if we gather a complete picture of all timelines before drawing any conclusions."

Ruarc lit a pipe with a practiced flick of his lighter, the flame illuminating his weathered face momentarily. He then puffed out rings of smoke that drifted lazily upward, curling into the air like ghostly apparitions. "The transformed nexus and multiple planets came after that timeline, right?" Ruarc asked, his brow furrowed in thought.

"Well, technically the counter timeline was in between the two," Aodhán interjected, his tone precise.

"Technicality aside, it would be good to discuss the transformed nexus," Oliver said, leaning forward slightly. "We'd actually come closer to forming an alliance then."

"And that wench got close enough to be able to communicate with you telepathically," Ruarc stated, his voice rising in anger before he slammed his fists on the table with a resonating thud. "She killed you!"

A flash of anger flickered across Oliver's eyes before a calm settled over him like a winter blanket. "We acted without her consent, connived, and manipulated the situation."

"So, we're not going to do that this time?" Aodhán asked, astonishment coloring his voice.

Oliver lifted his hands in exasperation, the gesture expressing a silent admission of past errors.

"Because it sure didn't seem like it in the counter world…as ghosts," Ruarc continued, his and Aodhán's questions volleying back and forth like a tense game of tennis.

"And they appeared to have attained powers in that ghost world," Aodhán added, his voice carrying a hint of intrigue.

"Yes, and more magic in the 1920s," Oliver conceded, a note of resignation in his voice. "Which is why we're reconvening before moving further forward as planned."

Oliver cradled his head in his hands, the weight of past mistakes pressing heavily upon him. Since the beginning of all this, he'd been going about it all wrong. Hopping on the reincarnation train with Mary had brought him insight throughout the timelines. He'd slipped back into his old military tactical protocol without a second thought.

Sending his counterparts to 1920, he'd lost his love again instead of achieving his revenge against her niece. Anna's heart had been just as large as Elizabeth's. Of course, she'd save Claudia. The fact that he hadn't seen how inevitable it had been haunted him still, a specter of regret that refused to be banished.

He should have recognized that sending his counters would create an echo world, a parallel existence reverberating with unintended consequences. The notion of becoming a ghost, a specter trapped between moments, was something he never could have predicted. How could he resist the urge to send his two closest allies back in time? They were seated before him even now, their presence a testament to his choices.

Yet, he had miscalculated with the altered helixes, and no counters had intervened then. The inability to locate his beloved, intertwined with an insatiable desire to preserve the world so he might find her, twisted his thoughts into a labyrinth of confusion. It wasn't so much that his reasoning was distorted; rather, it was as if this yearning stunted his growth, preventing him from evolving beyond his flawed intentions.

Instead of allowing the altered helixes to integrate naturally, he had intervened, strategically placing candidates he believed would not only serve as assets but also remain steadfastly loyal to his cause. In doing so, he shattered authenticity, trampling on the rights of others and suppressing the freedoms of anyone who dared oppose him.

He had wielded every tool at his disposal to amass power, but what had this relentless pursuit brought him? Death! Eventually, both he and his lover were cast out from the afterlife, granted the chance to reincarnate—a solitary act of redemption. In an attempt to thwart Brennan, Mary's love at the time, from reincarnating as well, he tried to take him along. But it was a futile gesture, too little, too late.

Despite this, the lesson eluded him. His frenzied madness persisted into the transformed nexus, where his adversary lay in wait. In his single-minded quest for victory, he lost focus, allowing himself to be consumed by the drive to win. With each battle he triumphed, his confidence swelled, and his vigilance waned, slipping away inch by inch.

She bided her time, enduring blow after blow while he grew increasingly exposed. Her hope was tenacious, a resilience he had never encountered before, as she patiently awaited the opportune moment.

"Hello!" Ruarc snapped his fingers in front of Oliver's face, pulling him back to the present. "You disappeared there for a bit."

"So what's the plan?" Aodhán inquired, curiosity etched in his features.

"I think Elizabeth died because of the curse on my family," Oliver replied, his voice tinged with the weight of revelation.

"Not this again," Ruarc huffed, his voice tinged with exasperation as he rubbed his temples.

"I haven't heard about this," Aodhán exclaimed, his eyebrows shooting up in shock, his eyes wide with disbelief.

"The Cromwell family is notoriously known for suffering under a curse," Cromwell began, his voice low and somber. "My lineage has been plagued by the early deaths of women and children, a misfortune that was greatly exacerbated by Thomas Cromwell's involvement in the execution of Anne Boleyn."

"But how do we combat a curse?" Ruarc asked, his tone a mix of curiosity and concern.

"I'll dispatch Elizabeth to recruit those skilled in Celtic magic," Cromwell replied, his eyes narrowing with determination. "Instead of sending her to gather military intelligence."

"Will that be enough?" Aodhán asked, his voice tinged with skepticism. "Or is further action required?"

"There is a reason I called this meeting," Cromwell said, his voice firm as he leaned forward.

Ruarc and Aodhán mirrored his movement, sensing that Cromwell was finally approaching the crux of the matter.

"We cannot permit our men to loot," Cromwell stated, his voice unwavering. "Citizens must be fully compensated for anything taken out of necessity."

"The men won't like that," Aodhán commented, a hint of warning in his voice.

"We'll proceed regardless," Cromwell replied resolutely.

"And how are we to acquire the funds for this?" Ruarc inquired, his brow furrowed in concern.

"We'll have to find a way," Cromwell asserted. "The artillery is delayed, and I would prefer to maintain our advantage."

"But won't the enemy attempt to raid us?" Aodhán asked, his voice edged with anxiety.

"I'm confident that can be managed," Cromwell assured him.

"So, we WILL get to engage some of them while we wait." Ruarc nodded, a glint of anticipation in his eyes.

Cromwell could feel the tenuous grip on the situation slipping through his fingers.

"How long must we endure waiting in tents?" Aodhán asked, a note of impatience creeping into his voice.

"I know, I know." Cromwell sighed. "Winter is approaching."

"They're bringing the demicannon with the artillery?" Ruarc asked, his eyebrows arching in astonishment.

"Of course, the wall will require larger cannonballs." Cromwell nodded, his voice steady with resolve.

"How many cannonballs?" Aodhán inquired, his tone edged with anticipation.

"Hundreds," Cromwell replied, his words hanging in the air like a promise of victory.

Both men exhaled deeply, relief washing over them with Cromwell's assurance.

"Be sure every man has a helmet," Cromwell continued, his gaze unwavering. "They'll be needed once we bring down that damn wall." His leather coat creaked softly as he tugged on the sleeves, smoothing out the wrinkles with practiced precision.

"We'll be prepared for the papist dogs," Ruarc declared with a huff, his breath visible in the chilly air.

"Do you really think Sir Arthur Aston's wooden leg is full of gold like they say?" Aodhán asked, curiosity dancing in his eyes.

Cromwell rolled his eyes, his patience thinning, while Ruarc allowed a small smile to play on his lips.

"It would be useful to make up for all the paying instead of looting," Ruarc commented, his voice tinged with irony.

"They should pay more than that, though—for their little rebellions," Aodhán spat out, bitterness lining his words.

"And what would you have done if your land had been seized?" Cromwell asked, his tone probing, eyes narrowing slightly.

"Careful," Ruarc warned. "You already appear sympathetic with the enemy given your wife's origin."

"Hold your tongue," Cromwell barked, his voice sharp as a blade.

As if on cue, the tent door lifted, and Cromwell was enveloped by the delicate scent of rosewater. The sight of his beloved Elizabeth stole his breath away; her presence a balm to his weary soul. Years they had been together, yet in his eyes, she remained untouched by time. There was always a light about her, an ethereal shine to her hair and a warm glow to her skin. In her presence, he was transported to a different world entirely—one filled with happiness and goodwill, with forgiveness and an all-encompassing warmth that banished the harsh realities of the outside world.

"Speak of the devil," Aodhán remarked, his tone dripping with irony.

"Get out," Cromwell commanded with a steely glare, his eyes fixed firmly on the men. They stomped out, their boots thudding heavily against the ground, leaving Cromwell alone with his wife in the dimly lit tent. Elizabeth approached him swiftly, wrapping her arms around him in a fierce embrace. Cromwell savored the warmth of the hug but reluctantly let his arms drop to his sides. She gently placed a rolled-up piece of parchment on the wooden table before him.

"The map as requested," Elizabeth said, her voice soft yet tinged with an underlying tension.

"Thank you, Dear. I know this must be hard for you, sharing information about your hometown with the enemy," Cromwell replied, his voice a mixture of gratitude and concern.

"I followed them in religious pursuits, and it cost us our child." She huffed, her emotions a turbulent storm beneath her composed exterior.

"It was no one's fault." Cromwell attempted to soothe her, though his thoughts drifted back to the shadow of his family curse. "We have plenty of healthy children at home," he reminded her gently.

"Still, I feel the loss every day, like a gaping hole inside me," Elizabeth confessed, her voice thick with sorrow.

Cromwell stood and wrapped her in another embrace, the fabric of her dress soft against his skin, wishing he could somehow absorb her pain. "I think you'll enjoy the next task," he murmured into her hair, his voice tender.

"The one we spoke about before?" she asked, curiosity piquing through her grief.

"No, something new," Cromwell replied with a hint of excitement.

"Oh?" Elizabeth questioned, raising an eyebrow.

"I need you to get closer to the Celtic magic doers," he exclaimed, a spark of intrigue in his eyes. "Perhaps you can see your sister. That always seems to cheer you up."

Elizabeth placed her thumb thoughtfully to her lip, a familiar gesture she often used when holding back information. Cromwell considered pressing her for more insight but decided against it, respecting her boundaries.

"How will that help you? If I were to go to the inn, I'd be able to get you more information. A garrison has gathered there," she suggested, her mind already calculating the possibilities.

"The plans have changed. We were meeting to discuss them just before you entered," Cromwell explained, his expression serious.

"If you say so," Elizabeth said, a hint of mischief in her voice as she kissed him farewell. A twinkle appeared in her eye, a sure sign of revelation. Before Cromwell could inquire further, she lifted the tent door and slipped out as quickly as she'd arrived, leaving him to ponder her newfound insight.

CHAPTER FIVE – CLAUDIA

"The connection's automatic, I'm in his mind, and he's in mine, but I'm the only one who has a clue of what's going on and any ability to control things in our space now." (Ghostly Howls)

Lately, memories of this place have been flooding back to me, and perhaps that's why its sight takes my breath away, it's stunningly beautiful. I follow the familiar path toward the hawthorn tree nearest our family cottage, watching as shadows spill between the trees. My leg muscles tense with each step; my balance still hasn't fully returned since my time traveling. I suspect that my lingering imbalance is due to a damaged cochlea, though it might also be the rush of adrenaline from the excitement of reuniting with family, especially seeing Elizabeth.

A thin wisp of smoke curls from the chimney, a clear sign that there is life inside. I reflect on all the places I have once called home through the ages. The geraniums and poppies around me now bring to mind the hydrangeas and daffodils that once adorned the pergola outside our first home after the 1920s timeline. I find myself wishing that Vex and Kitchen—mechanical assistants who became like friends—were here with me now, though I'd probably really stick out then.

In both those timelines, my dad had been missing just as he was in 1920. In one, he sent me a warning message to be cautious; in another, he risked his life to protect others. I try to recall what he was like in 1649, but those memories have become fuzzy. It doesn't matter much, though—I'll be seeing him again soon enough.

As I draw near, an overwhelming silence falls around me. A seed of doubt begins to creep in—maybe no one is here, and they simply left the fire burning to warm the cabin—but I push it aside. A shadow darts at the edge of my vision. I turn quickly, my heart pounding, only to find nothing there. The wind rustles through the grass, and goosebumps prick my arms while tiny flickers, resembling floating dust motes, invade my sight. I take a deep breath, trying to steady myself.

Gathering all my resolve, I move toward the cabin. Its slightly off-kilter, almost natural appearance strikes me as endearing—like it had grown from the earth itself. The quirky, wavy roof even brings a smile to my face. Standing at the door, I run my fingers through my hair in an effort to tame the windblown mess. As I reach for the doorknob, I notice a wrinkle in my sleeve and smooth it out. My heart races as I grasp the knob, but before I can fully touch it, it turns on its own.

"I'm lost," I blurt out, my voice quivering as my dad nearly collides with me, his eyes wide with stark terror. I struggle violently to keep from leaping forward and engulfing him in a desperate hug. It feels as if the air has been stolen from my lungs; suddenly my head spins, and I teeter on the brink of collapse.

"Oh dear," he murmurs, his hands clutching my arms like anchors, holding me steady. "Are you all right, Miss?"

"I'm Claudia," I rasp, barely managing the words through a tremor. "I'm lost."

From behind him, Mary—my own mother from 1649—emerges, her face contorted with fierce concern. "What do we have here? Bring her inside. The poor thing looks ravaged by hunger."

Barnabus rushes me into the foyer and seats me in a creaking chair. "I'm Barnabus and this is my wife, Mary," he declares, his gesture firm toward her.

Mary dampens a cloth and presses it to my forehead. "And this is my sister, Elizabeth." She points to the corner.

"What did you mean when you said you're lost?" Elizabeth demands—I recognize her voice, a soul I'd identify anywhere, though I didn't always. My aunt!

"Yeah, um, I need to get to town," I confess, my tone a chaotic blend of nonchalance and raw anxiety. My emotions ricochet violently. I can tell she knows I'm hiding something but also that I'm anxious.

"Here, have something to drink," Mary offers, extending a cup of pure, untainted well water. The simple act of her care resurrects echoes of childhood when comfort was an embrace away. I sip the cool liquid, and its clarity steadies my tortured nerves, as if imbued with both maternal warmth and a hint of ancient magic.

"Thank you," I manage, exhaling a shaky sigh.

"Where did you come from?" Elizabeth asks. "You seemed frightened, as if you'd been chased by faeries."

"Just a bit seasick from my travels," I reply, my voice gathering strength. "I've been camped in the woods, desperate for more supplies."

Barnabus interjects with a grave warning, "You must be careful in those woods—there are places best left undisturbed."

Without missing a beat, Elizabeth cuts in, "I'm headed that way myself. I can take you with me." Her offer hangs in the air, potent and laced with an unspoken promise.

"That would be wonderful," I murmur, taking another trembling sip as a fragile hope steadies my resolute heart.

"Where exactly have you camped?" Mary inquires, her voice tender but edged with alarm. "Will you be seeking refuge in town?"

"I'm merely out for supplies today," I answer, trying to smooth the raw edges of my worry.

Elizabeth's eyes flash with a stern warning as she shoots Mary a glance of dismay, shaking her head in regret, knowing her sister is about to ignore the urgent caution.

"You'll stay with us then," Mary declares firmly, "at least until you're safely settled."

At first, the thought of being reunited with those I've lost fills me with warmth, like the gentle embrace of a cherished memory. But soon, the warmth twists into worry as I envision the desperation Alex would feel if I failed to return to the cave.

"I don't mind sleeping under the stars, but I greatly appreciate your offer," I say, offering a smile of gratitude.

"Stop for dinner after you've been to town then?" Barnabus suggests, and I can't suppress the smile that blooms across my face like a flower in the sun.

"Of course. That sounds wonderful," I reply, the anticipation of a shared meal brightening my spirits.

"We best be on our way then in order to make it back in time," Elizabeth advises. With that, we begin our journey, the path now cloaked in a delicate mist that hovers like a whispered secret. Dew-kissed geraniums and poppies line our route, their vibrant colors softened by the moisture. Above us, birds serenade the morning with cheerful notes, a symphony of nature echoing through the air.

In this life, Elizabeth is a striking figure, tall and willowy, with long, silky dark hair that cascades down her back like a flowing river. Her eyes are a mesmerizing shade of hazel, capturing all the colors of the world like a prism. As we walk, sun rays peek through the canopy above, casting dappled light on our path.

"Why do you really insist on camping out?" Elizabeth inquires, her voice curious yet gentle.

"There may or may not be a young man involved," I confess, the truth slipping out before I can restrain it. Something about her presence draws honesty from me like water from a well.

She stoops to pick up a small pebble on the path, turning it thoughtfully in her hand. "Is that why you traveled away from home? For love?" she asks, her tone light yet probing.

A blush creeps into my cheeks, and though she doesn't know it, while I came here with someone I'm falling for, her love was the deciding factor. "Yes," I admit, my voice barely above a whisper.

She tosses the pebble against a tree, watching as it ricochets off another with a soft, repetitive clatter. The act seems to be one of habit, a familiar rhythm in an unpredictable world. "I can get that. Running away from family to be with the one you love," she muses, her words resonating with unspoken understanding.

While that's not exactly it, I seize the opportunity, sensing she's opening up to me. "It sounds as if you speak from experience," I venture, hoping to prompt further sharing.

"Yes, my family does not approve of my love," she reveals, her voice tinged with a quiet defiance.

I wait for more, but silence envelops us once again. My attention is drawn to a tree beside the path, stark against the landscape—lightning-struck and charred, yet resilient. Its trunk bears the scars of nature's fury, yet it stands tall, reaching for the sky with unwavering determination. Leaves sprout defiantly from a branch, a testament to survival against all odds.

As Drogheda comes into view, the town materializing from the mist, further words elude me, my thoughts consumed by the adventure ahead.

"Impressive, isn't it?" Elizabeth asks, her voice carrying a hint of wonder.

"It is," I reply, as memories start to flood back with each step we take.

"You'll be wanting the mercantile for supplies," she suggests, her eyes scanning the bustling scene.

I nod, my gaze lingering on the towering walls made of massive masonry that loom over us like ancient sentinels. As we step through the entrance, a steady stream of townspeople flows past us, the loud chatter and the clatter of products creating a lively hum. I absorb every detail with awe; it feels like stepping into another time, another world—yet it's all strangely familiar. Each building we pass stirs a sense of recognition within me, like pieces of a long-forgotten puzzle falling into place.

A cluster of men gathers outside a weathered inn, capturing Elizabeth's attention. Their voices are low and conspiratorial. She might be able to hear what they're saying, but it's impossible for me.

"What is it?" I ask, sensing her intrigue.

"There's been talk of a garrison forming," she replies, her voice tinged with concern.

Oh, no. My heart sinks at the realization—she's spying for Cromwell, exactly the kind of entanglement we don't need. My thoughts are abruptly interrupted by the joyful sound of young laughter. Elizabeth's eyes widen, and I follow her gaze to see a cherubic toddler with golden curls darting between the men, playing tag with infectious glee. Elizabeth instinctively steps toward them, and I feel compelled to gently grasp her arm.

"I only want to greet the child. I won't be but a minute," she assures me.

But as we move in that direction, a pair of townswomen intercept us, their faces bright with recognition.

"Elizabeth, it's good to see you!" exclaims a woman with strawberry blonde hair, her eyes sparkling with warmth. Her dress is impeccably tailored, with extra ribbon adding a fashionable flair.

"Yes, how have you been?" the second woman inquires, her auburn hair cascading around her jovial face like a warm halo. Her smile, vibrant and full of life, radiates infectious energy.

"I'm well," Elizabeth replies warmly. "Just showing Claudia the way to the mercantile. She's new to town and in need of supplies."

"Oh, then you must come to the gathering tomorrow," suggests the woman with strawberry blonde hair, her voice inviting and enthusiastic. "I'm Fidelma."

"Yes, you'll be able to meet so many people and get acquainted with our town," adds the woman with the auburn locks. "It's a pleasure. I'm Líadan." She extends her hand, her eyes twinkling with friendliness.

As I clasp her hand, a cascade of visions floods my mind, vivid and consuming. I see the gathering planned for the following day: people twirling and dancing under strings of lights, and in a quiet corner, Fidelma and Líadan share a tender kiss. Words of gratitude and response to their kindness escape me as the visions overwhelm my senses.

"Are you okay?" Elizabeth's hands are suddenly on my cheeks, her touch gentle yet grounding, pulling me back from the foggy depths of my mind.

"She has the sight," Líadan observes, her tone both curious and certain. Though I don't fully grasp the meaning, the three women exchange a look of silent understanding and agreement.

"You look like you could use the walk to the mercantile to clear your head," Elizabeth suggests softly, her gaze filled with concern.

I manage only a nod and a tentative smile at the women I've just met, my breath slowly returning to a steady rhythm.

Once my breathing is calm, I ask, "What did she mean—I have the sight?"

"It was something she sensed, is all," Elizabeth reassures me, her voice gentle. "If you do have the sight, it's a gift."

"When our hands met, visions overtook me, but I've never experienced anything like that before. Are you sure it's not Líadan?" I question, still bewildered.

Elizabeth's hand moves to cover her mouth, eyes wide with realization. "No, Líadan doesn't have the sight. Perhaps your soul is connected to this place—it's awakened your magic."

The thought sends a shiver down my spine. Could this reveal too much about me?

"Nothing to worry about," Elizabeth adds with a comforting smile. "We can work with you—help you control it."

She halts and pivots toward the building beside us, her eyes lingering on the familiar facade. "The mercantile," she announces, her voice a gentle invitation. I anticipate she'll leave me here, resuming her daily routine, but instead, she steps inside with me, the wooden door creaking softly in welcome.

"Tell me about yourself," I implore, hoping her words will serve as a balm to my restless mind. "Distract me from my thoughts."

"You already know that I left my home to be with the one I love," she begins, her voice warm with remembrance.

"And was it worth it?" I ask, searching her face for the truth.

A soft smile graces her lips. "Yes, we have a wonderful life together." Yet, the smile dims, a shadow passing over her features. "Of course, we've faced hardships too, just like everybody else."

Gently, I place a comforting hand on her shoulder, feeling the weight of her past.

"We lost one of our children, and it nearly broke me—us," she confesses, her voice quivering with emotion as she brushes away a stray tear. "You actually remind me of our lost child in a way."

Moved by her vulnerability, I embrace her, unable to withstand the sorrow etched in her eyes. The depth of her loss and despair is overwhelming.

"My husband fought against the absolute power of the monarchy," she continues, her voice steadying. "I agreed with him that decisions should be made by the people. But after we lost our child, he lost sight a little. It's as if now he believes people should be forced into certain beliefs."

"And what do you believe?" I inquire, keen to understand her perspective.

"I believe fighting should be avoided at all costs," she replies, her conviction clear. "That people should be intelligent enough to negotiate and debate with their minds, not with violence."

The linen bag Marie had provided, now filled with the supplies, hangs heavily at my side as we make our way to the front of the store to pay. Thankfully, Mother also purchased coins from a collector before traveling back in time.

"That makes sense to me," I finally respond to Elizabeth, her ideals resonating within me.

She offers a warm smile. "It looks like you're all set here. I need to run some errands too. Can you find your way back?"

"Yes," I assure her. "Does Drogheda have a library?"

"Not yet," she replies, "but the shop at the corner has some books. Anything you're looking for in particular?"

"There's nothing particular—it's just that without a good book to read, I don't feel complete." Her eyes light up again, and I feel a sense of relief knowing that our separate paths are for the best. At the corner shop, I delight in the vast collection of books. The shelves are filled with the expected titles—Shakespeare, Cervantes, Milton—but tucked away in a quiet corner, I discover a book that resembles a handmade journal. Its allure is irresistible. When I open it, I learn it's a local volume on magic and our cultural history before England set out to erase it. I eagerly pore over the pages, searching for any reference to possessing the sight. The book is packed with valuable information. Eventually, I lift my eyes from my seat and notice that darkness is beginning to fall outside.

I make a hasty return to the cottage.

"But we've already finished dinner," Barnabus remarks. "We're relieved you're safe—we were really worried."

"Are you sure you don't want to stay the night?" Mary asks.

"Sister, she already said no," Elizabeth interjects. "Don't make her repeat herself."

"Just let me pack some food for you, at least," Mary insists. "I won't take no for an answer."

"Will you be joining us for tomorrow's gathering?" Elizabeth inquires.

"I'd love to. Thank you so much for everything."

The deepening darkness ushers me onto the path back toward the cave, where a crisp, cold breeze races across my skin, setting my heart aflutter as if touched by a surge of unseen magic. My pace quickens as an inexplicable sense of foreboding washes over me. In the nearly impenetrable blackness, a vague, shadowy figure emerges, darting toward me. I stand frozen, the world narrowing into that singular, surreal moment, when suddenly the figure collides with me, and a palpable energy hums under my skin.

"Claudia?" comes the sound of a familiar voice, and at that moment, a rich blend of scents—a heady mix of wet woods and rain—swirls in the air, evoking memories not of Drogheda but of rain-soaked evenings in Kansas City. Alex pulls me into an embrace that speaks of both familiarity and urgent need. As he holds me tight, his kisses begin softly, dusting my face with gentle affection and gradually building to claim my mouth. My pulse quickens, not from fear this time, but from an undeniable, fierce desire. In the heat of our kiss, visions and wild possibilities flood my mind, blurring the line between his thoughts—perhaps glimpses of "the sight"—and the stirrings of my own passion. His hand finds its way to my waist, a gesture charged with both tenderness and yearning, while his other hand wraps securely around the back of my neck. The warmth that blooms beneath his touch sends shivers along my skin. Clasping his arms tightly, I yield to the moment as his thumb caresses the soft skin under my ear, and our kiss deepens into an insistent, fervent dance of hearts and souls.

CHAPTER SIX – ALEXANDER

"Something stinging pulls through my heart like a vine full of thorns dragged through my arteries. If this was just a battle or decoy as my enemies keep labelling things, the war is happening in my mind with condescending thoughts as ammo. The thing closest to my brain is the organ pumping warmth to it. My heart belongs to Vienna. Where is she?" (Omitted Pieces)

I stepped beneath the towering entrance of the woods, feeling a heavy mix of relief and dread ripple through me. The road behind me had given way to shadowed paths, and as I ventured further, darkness seemed to wrap the forest in its cold embrace. I spotted a broad oak tree looming nearby, its gnarled roots snaking across the ground like ancient fingers. I squinted at the bark, trying to place it in memory as if it were a signpost from my planned route. The silvery glow of the moon fought through the canopy, casting eerie, shifting patterns and highlighting the intricate network of roots that stirred bygone recollections.

A fragment of my research surfaced in a hushed whisper inside my mind: this very oak was sacred, a symbol of strength and wisdom, and linked to the power of Dagda. That knowledge lit a spark of hope—it could steer me toward the hidden cave I sought.

As I gazed deeper into the forest, the sudden snap of a branch shattered the silence. My heart jolted, and instinct took over; I crouched low among the underbrush. Although there was no specific threat in view, I knew that soldiers—whether friends or foes—strode these lands, and their reactions to an unexpected figure like me were always unpredictable.

I scanned the murky depths until a fleeting shadow caught my attention. Without a moment's hesitation, I sprang silently after it, eager to unravel its mystery. Each stride was a battle against nature itself; low-hanging branches whipped at my face while brittle twigs threatened to betray my stealth. Then, as if conjured by some otherworldly spirit, long, flowing hair trailed behind the dark figure. I halted mid-stride, transfixed by the ethereal sight. Legends spoke of a faery's gaze, capable of ensnaring a soul in a trance—whisking one away to a hidden mansion while leaving nothing but a log behind. In my mind's eye, I could almost hear the tinkling strains of faery music mingling with the rustle of leaves.

Shaking my head as if to dislodge the surreal image, I found the shadow had vanished. Had it melted into the trees, or was it now tracking my every move, silently waiting to act? I moved forward with cautious, measured steps, straining to regain my bearings. A cool breeze stirred the leaves overhead, carrying with it an aroma that combined the earthy scent of oak with a spicy, almond-like tang.

Hawthorn petals danced around me in the gust, and once more, an almost imperceptible melody wove through the air— a high-pitched harp tune that began sweet and clear before merging into a relentless, ringing cacophony, much like the tinnitus Claudia had once described in detail. I pressed my hands over my ears, scrunching my eyes in a futile bid to shut out the maddening sound.

When at last I dared to open my eyes again, the shadow had reappeared. I blinked rapidly, trying to discern its shape through the dim light, until recognition struck me. Without thinking, I broke into a sprint toward her, only to collide headfirst with Claudia. "Claudia?" I gasped, steadying her to prevent a fall, my heart pounding as I searched her face for answers in the perplexing silence of the forest.

Pulling her in close, I gently ran my hands over her back and arms, feeling the reassuring smoothness of her skin to ensure she was unharmed. The absence of any bruises or cuts brought a wave of relief that washed over me. I pressed my lips to hers repeatedly, caught up in a rush of exhilaration. Soon, our kisses became fervent, as urgent as the roar of a plane accelerating down the runway.

Almost every part of me yearned to continue kissing Claudia, but a tiny voice in my mind reminded me of the need to return to the cave before darkness fully descended. "Do you know how to get back to the cave?" I asked, reluctantly breaking the kiss and pulling away just an inch.

"I believe it's this way," she replied confidently, pointing past the silhouette of a hawthorn tree. Her other arm remained draped around my shoulders, a comforting weight.

I glanced upward, searching for familiar constellations that could guide us on our path. Her playful pout caught my attention. "You don't trust my sense of direction?" she teased, giving my arm a gentle tug. "Remember, I've been here before." Her wink was filled with mischievous assurance.

Fortunately, my own assessment confirmed her directions, but I kept that to myself, responding with a wink of my own.

As we walked through the forest, I held her hand tightly. Her fingers traced gentle patterns on my forearm, sending my heart into an erratic rhythm. She leaned into me, and I instinctively wrapped my arm over her shoulders, pulling her closer. Her warmth seeped into me, blanketing my heart with a comforting heat.

"Were you successful today?" I asked, pressing a kiss to the top of her head, savoring the scent of her hair.

"Yes and no," she replied, her voice laced with a smile. I could feel the curve of her lips against my biceps.

"What does that mean?" I inquired, curious.

"I met my family and connected," she said, turning her face up toward mine. The moonlight sparkled in her eyes, illuminating the depth of her emotions. "But we're going to have to keep a better eye on Elizabeth."

"Oh?" I murmured, brushing a kiss against Claudia's cheek.

"Yes, she's as strong-willed as ever," Claudia continued, a note of admiration mixed with concern in her voice. "It's going to be nearly impossible to keep her out of the battle."

"Strong-willed, huh," I responded with a teasing grin. "Definitely doesn't run in the family."

"Hey!" She playfully thumped my arm with just enough force to make me chuckle.

The thought of battle spurred my steps, and I glanced sideways, worried Claudia might lag behind. But she kept pace effortlessly, her long, elegant legs matching my stride with ease. My mind wandered, and I couldn't help but imagine those legs bare, beautifully defined with gentle curves that would drive any man to distraction.

"Finally," Marie exclaimed, her voice echoing as we stepped into the cool, shadowy cave.

"I brought us some dinner," Claudia quickly interjected, her voice light and cheerful to divert her mother's intense gaze from the questions she was gearing up to ask.

As we settled down to eat, Marie began to outline the events that had led us to the brink of this siege.

"Oliver's army arrived from the south today," Marie said, her voice steady but laced with urgency. "They've pitched their tents on the slope opposite the town. The artillery has not arrived yet."

"How much time do we have?" I asked, my mind racing with possibilities and plans.

"We have a few days," Marie replied, and I noticed Claudia let out an audible sigh of relief, her shoulders relaxing slightly.

While I was glad to see her relieved, a sudden worry took root in my mind. If I'm at the dock with my new friends when Cromwell's army strikes, I'll have no choice but to join the battle. I should probably brush up on swordsmanship and mentally run through every military tactic I know.

Marie rummaged through her bag, the sound of rustling fabric breaking the silence. Eventually, she pulled out a few small chains that caught the flickering torchlight, casting tiny reflections onto the cave walls. She handed two to Claudia. "One is for you to wear for protection. Please give the other to Elizabeth."

"How am I supposed to," Claudia began, her voice faltering. "I mean, what should I say?"

I gently placed my hand on her forearm, offering reassurance. "Something will come to you."

Claudia twirled the triquetra pendant hanging from the chain between her fingers, its intricate loops glinting softly as she pondered her next move.

"I have one for you too, Alex." Marie extended her hand toward me, revealing a triquetra pendant hanging from a rough, woven rope. The intricate Celtic knot gleamed under the dim light. "I figured you could tie it to your clothes if you don't want to wear it around your neck."

I threaded the pendant carefully through my belt, feeling the cool metal against my fingers.

As I secured it, Claudia let out a soft gasp, her eyes widening in appreciation. "Elizabeth helped me today, so I can offer the necklace as a gift of gratitude," Claudia explained, her voice warm and sincere.

"That sounds wonderful," Marie replied, her hands busy gathering her belongings. "I'm planning to sleep in a little alcove down the way toward the exit."

"Oh?" Claudia raised an eyebrow, curiosity piqued.

"Yeah, there's a skylight that I want to fall asleep under. The stars are incredible tonight."

"Goodnight," Claudia said, wrapping her arms around Marie in a gentle hug.

As Marie departed, Claudia intertwined her fingers with mine, her touch sending a spark up my arm. She led me to our cozy alcove, a space just big enough for the two of us. The soft rustle of leaves and the distant chirping of crickets created a peaceful score.

As we settled down, I reached out, brushing her hair behind her ears with tender fingers. Her eyes met mine, a soft smile playing on her lips, and my heart swelled.

Pulling her closer, I felt my heart pounding like a relentless drum. Her warmth seeped into me, a comforting heat that spread through my body. Her lips met mine, soft and inviting. She wrapped her arms around my neck, pulling me into a deeper kiss. I kissed back, savoring the gentle pressure of her lips against mine. Her fingers traced a path down my neck, sending shivers across my skin.

Claudia tilted her head, capturing my bottom lip between hers, teasing it with a playful suck before gently nipping with her teeth. Our kisses grew urgent, fervent, as if the adrenaline from our earlier adventure in the woods had found its way into this moment—desire coursing through my veins.

Her leg curled over my hip, pulling me closer. Her touch was all-consuming, a dizzying mix of tenderness and intensity.

Her tongue danced with mine, stealing every coherent thought from my mind. A wave of heat surged through me, setting my skin ablaze as her lips traveled to my neck.

When she pulled back, I couldn't help but continue our previous actions, pressing my lips to her neck. The soft moan she released was intoxicating, and I fought the urge to tear away the fabric separating us. I placed a steadying hand on her chest, inhaling deeply to calm the storm within.

"We should stop," I whispered, my voice barely steady.

"Why?" Claudia asked, her bottom lip curling into a pout, her voice a mix of curiosity and concern.

I inhaled deeply, letting the air fill my lungs to steady the whirlwind of emotions threatening to break loose. Claudia's eyes, wide and searching, locked onto mine as she shook her head, bracing herself as if ready to counter whatever I had to say. I pulled her into a warm embrace, feeling her slight tremor against my chest. The faint sound of her sniffle reached my ears, and I gently leaned back to meet her gaze. Her eyes glistened, a hint of moisture pooling at the corners. Was she crying? Tenderly, I brought her hand to my lips and pressed a kiss against her palm, feeling the warmth of her skin.

"What is it?" she asked, her voice barely above a whisper, cracking slightly with emotion.

"I want us to be wed before we…" I began, my voice trailing off as the words hung between us.

A slow, radiant smile began to spread across her face, lighting up her features.

"What?" I stammered, a small, self-conscious laugh escaping my lips.

"We have been married," she replied, shaking her head softly, as if amused by a secret only she knew. "It was a different timeline, but we were married."

Visions from other timelines had been surfacing in my mind lately, fleeting and elusive. I searched my memory, hoping to catch a glimpse of our union. She seemed to sense my struggle and offered a gentle nudge.

"There were white folding chairs adorned with satin ties lining the aisle at our wedding," she described, her voice filled with nostalgia.

"Tell me more," I urged, eager to grasp the fragments of the past...well, future. Timelines are confusing.

"The light from the stained glass window above us cast a moonlike glow throughout the room. There were white floral decorations everywhere, and the deep, resonant notes of an organ filled the air," she continued, painting the picture with her words.

"Keep going," I encouraged, leaning into the warmth of her recollection.

"All our friends were there. When you saw me, you smiled nervously at first," she added, her eyes dancing with the memory.

That brought a smile to my face. The image of her, radiant and breathtaking, began to take shape in my mind.

"You comforted me like no one else could," she said, her voice soft with emotion.

Bits and pieces of the memory began to coalesce—her hair cascading around her shoulders, the gentle curve of her smile, the sweetness of our kiss. "I'm remembering," I said, the realization dawning on me.

"See, we were married," she affirmed, her voice filled with certainty.

She leaned in to kiss me, her lips soft and inviting, and ran her fingers through my hair, sending shivers down my spine. I traced a line of kisses along her jaw, slowly moving toward her ear and back down to her shoulder blade. She inhaled sharply, her breath catching as I explored the contours of her skin. Her leg hooked over my hip, and she rocked gently into me. "Claudia!" I gasped, as her nimble fingers began to undo my buttons. I fumbled with the delicate lace of her dress, loosening it to reveal the warmth beneath. Our lips met again, and she arched into me, her body pressing close. My hand found her thigh, and a deep, primal sensation surged through me. Waves of pleasure washed over us, a relentless tide that we surrendered to, blissfully lost in each other.

Guarded Time

CHAPTER SEVEN – MARIE

Let's delve into how things remain constant over time, with subtle transformations. I'm standing in the dimly lit kitchen, the air thick with the scent of melting tallow, alongside Róis, Onóra, Neasa, and Étaín. In years to come, people will melt paraffin instead, the process becoming industrialized and efficient.

"Would you like one?" Róis asks, extending her hand with a strip of material. Her nose is covered with another strip, wrapped snugly around her head. "I've infused it with lavender for a soothing scent," she explains.

"Róis can't stand the smell," Étaín comments, gesturing toward the bubbling pot of tallow.

"And she's thoughtful enough to consider if others might be bothered too," Onóra adds, her tone appreciative.

"Thank you!" I say, reaching for the offered material, but then Neasa interjects.

"You don't have to take it if the smell doesn't trouble you, Laura," Neasa remarks, her voice gentle.

Pulling my hand back, I respond, "It doesn't bother me, actually, but I appreciate the gesture."

"Would you like to help me organize the rushes?" Neasa asks, her arms brimming with the long, slender plants.

As I help her lay them out meticulously on the wooden table, I inquire, "Why is the festival earlier this year?" I hope this question will bolster my cover as someone less informed.

"We need to prepare for a possible attack," Onóra replies, placing a comforting hand on my shoulder, her eyes serious.

I glance around, searching for Étaín, but she has slipped away. Concerned, I ask, "Will the harvest be sufficient to keep everyone fed? For how long will it last?"

"I have the seeds," Étaín's voice rings out as she reenters the room, carrying a small burlap sack. "Conor brought them by," she adds, her tone light.

"Such a good young man," Neasa remarks, her eyes softening. "Even if he can be as prickly as you."

Étaín playfully nudges Neasa with her hip, and they burst into laughter, a sound that fills the room with warmth. It's one of those countless, unrecorded moments in history that define the essence of human life.

"I'll bring my panflute to aid in Banbha's blessing," Róis chimes in, her voice full of enthusiasm, prompting a quick shush from Étaín.

"What?" Onóra exclaims, shooting Étaín an exasperated glance. "Do you imagine Englishmen are lurking just outside, hanging on to our every word like spies?"

"You can't be too careful," Étaín counters, her voice laced with caution.

"We know," Neasa murmurs, placing her hands reassuringly on Étaín's shoulders. "It's just so hard to remain so restrained for such a long time."

"The tallow's ready to dip the rush in," I say, breaking the spell of the moment with a hint of reluctance. They exchange stories from the past, their voices weaving a tapestry of nostalgia as we submerge the wicks into the warm, melted tallow repeatedly, the process familiar and soothing. The rich, earthy scent of the tallow fills the air, and as I watch the layers build on each wick, I am transported. Each dip feels like a step back in time, and for a fleeting moment, it seems as though I have never left this era.

"I can't believe you invited him," Étaín says, her voice laced with accusation as she narrows her eyes at Onóra. "He's always so grumpy. Every time I see him, he looks like he's just bitten into a lemon."

"Maybe he's grumpy because no one ever invites him to the festival," Onóra retorts, her cheeks flushed with defensiveness as she crosses her arms tightly over her chest.

"Do any of you feel a small negative feeling under the joy?" Neasa asks, her eyes scanning the crowd as if searching for the source of an invisible tension.

"I hope it goes away in time," I say, glancing around at the vibrant decorations. "I mean, just look at how beautiful we've made the place."

The beautiful pink firewood wildflowers hang gracefully from every available surface, their petals a soft splash of color against the dark wood. Candles flicker with a gentle, romantic glow along the tables, casting warm shadows that dance across the scene. The air is thick with the mouthwatering aroma of food being prepared for the feast, spices and herbs mingling into an irresistible scent.

The atmosphere stirs my memories of the first time I was here, the vivid recollection of events and arrivals swirling in my mind. It's good I remember, so I can steer clear of Barnabus, Mary, and Elizabeth when they show up.

"I hope so too," Onóra adds, her voice softer now, tinged with hope.

The gentle strains of harp music fill the air as the dancers clear space on the floor. The melody weaves a story of life and love, rich in cultural heritage. It's reminiscent of the olden days when even the Brehons would intone the law in a recitative chant to harp music, seated high on an eminence in the open air, while people gathered round to listen.

As more guests filter in, the music swells, and lively chatter surrounds us, a symphony of merriment and light-heartedness. The worry seems to have faded from Neasa's eyes. Onóra skillfully slices meat for the young boy sitting beside her, her hands steady and practiced. Étaín throws her head back with a jovial laugh at a joke shared by the man next to her. Róis's smile is accompanied by a shy blush, her cheeks as pink as the flowers.

It's a shame I have to leave, but I know Barnabus will be arriving soon. I bury my face in my hands, feeling the importance of avoiding an encounter.

"Are you okay?" Onóra asks, her voice gentle with concern.

"I have a splitting headache," I murmur, pressing my fingers to my temples as if to keep my skull from fracturing.

"Will you be all right?" Neasa asks, her voice laced with genuine concern as she peers at me through the dim lighting.

"Think I'm going to call it a night," I reply, like the throb in my head were intensifying with each beat of the music.

"But the festivities have just begun," Étaín protests, gesturing toward the lively crowd whose laughter and chatter fill the air.

"I have Valerian from the tincture shop back home," Róis offers, her hand resting gently on my arm. "Want me to go get it?"

"No, but may I grab some on my way out?" I ask, grateful for her kindness.

"Of course," she assures me with a nod.

As I make my way toward the exit, I notice two men loitering near the trail, their silhouettes partially concealed by the night's shadows. I rack my brain but find no recollection of their faces. An eerie aura seems to trail behind them like a phantom cloak. Instinctively, I duck behind the nearest oak tree, my heart pounding so violently that it drowns out their mumbled conversation as they pass just a few feet away.

The oak tree provides a solid, reassuring presence against my back, its rough bark grounding me in the moment. The darkness envelops me, and the crowd's focus is elsewhere, allowing me a covert vantage point from which I can observe the scene. I bide my time, waiting for the right moment to approach Claudia once she arrives and warn her of the unsettling presence I've just encountered.

Gradually, the tremors in my hands subside, and I draw in deep breaths, letting the fear dissipate with each exhalation. Two counters are here! I thought our mission was solely to save Elizabeth, but it seems Cromwell's machinations are at play once more, threatening to unravel everything.

Why would he want to stop us from saving his love? Does he want to claim the glory for himself? But how can he manage that when he's busy orchestrating a siege? How can he possibly juggle all these tasks simultaneously? Is that the purpose of the counters' presence?

My gaze drifts upwards, and I notice the sky teeming with ravens, their harsh caws echoing—an ominous harbinger of death. A chill wraps around me, and I feel every muscle in my body tighten, my jaw clenching as if bound by invisible wires. Mary's voice—my own voice—floats down the path, electrifying my senses.

I spot Claudia and feel a strong urge to rush to her, but I'm rooted in place as Barnabus and Mary lead the procession. Claudia and Elizabeth follow closely, flanked by two women adorned in elegant attire, Fidelma and Líadan, as stylish as ever. Their lighthearted conversation falters as they, too, glance at the ravens. Fear flickers across Líadan's face, and I know she senses it—the foreboding that hangs heavy in the air. Perhaps we'll gain new allies in this unsettling time.

As I bide my time, waiting for the right moment, I notice Alex arriving with Conor, Liam, and Rí. Their laughter and youthful exuberance momentarily stir a pang of envy within me. Though they're grown men, their energy is vibrant and full of life.

I bend down, pick up a small pebble, and toss it at Alex's shoe as they draw near. He pauses, glancing in my direction.

"I'm going to take a quick piss," he announces to his companions. "Meet you inside."

"Watch out for the faeries!" Liam shouts back with a laugh.

Alex lingers by the tree, eyeing his friends as they disappear into the festival.

"Is everything okay?" he asks, concern etched on his face.

"The counters are inside, and I need you to warn Claudia," I reply urgently.

"I thought I spotted one at the docks," Alex admits, a mixture of relief at his sanity and worry for Claudia playing across his features.

"See the two men by the harp," I say, pointing discreetly toward them. The harp's strings shimmer in the moonlight as a soft melody drifts through the air.

"Wait, but neither of them is the man at the dock who had an aura stream. Are there three now?" His brow furrows in confusion, eyes darting between the men.

"I don't think Cromwell's capable of that," I reply, my voice tinged with doubt. "In any case, please go warn Claudia."

"Yes, right." He nods with determination and dashes into the festival, his initial urgency betraying any attempt at subtlety. As he merges with the crowd, he slows his pace, blending into the throng of revelers.

He approaches Claudia, wrapping her in a warm embrace, their familiarity now exposed to the world. They'll have to maintain the truth of a couple in public now. Alex positions himself strategically, shielding her from the view of the counters like a protective barrier. Maybe their increased closeness will have its advantages.

They mingle with the festival-goers, feigning normalcy, though my nerves remain taut. I can't shake the thought of three counters. Could such a thing be possible? How would Cromwell manage it? The mystery of how he achieved even two counters unsettles me.

As time drags on, my feet grow numb, the cold seeping through my boots. I spot Alex and his friends nearing the exit, their faces flushed from hours of dancing, seemingly tireless.

Suddenly, Alex halts, doubling over and clamping his hands over his ears. His friends freeze, concern etched on their faces.

"Are you okay?" Rí asks, eyes wide with worry.

Alex straightens, lowering his hands slowly. "There was a loud ringing in my ears. It's gone now."

A deep horn echoes through the night, resonating like a summons.

"A ship's come in," Conor announces, urgency in his voice. "We have to go."

Alex rushes to Claudia, plants a quick kiss on her cheek, and then sprints after his friends, a blur of intensity.

A few men from the town garrison trail behind them, their expressions serious. One glances at his companion, murmuring, "Sasanachs?"

Claudia emerges, her presence a quiet strength. Alex must have told her I was here. "Mom," she whispers, yet it pierces the air like a shout.

"I had to warn you about the counters," I explain, my voice steady despite the chaos around us.

"Got it, Mom. There's no need for you to stay out here. Go home." Her words are firm but caring.

As she heads back inside, the counters stride out, crossing her path. One brushes past her roughly, sending her stumbling sideways. "Jerk!" I mutter under my breath, anger flaring at the disrespect.

They don't stop but continue onward, urgency in their stride. Claudia's face flickers between awareness and a blank stare, her expression shifting as if she's teetering on the edge of a vision. Her eyes are distant, half here, half elsewhere, lost in something I can't see.

I inch forward, my curiosity piqued, but retreat quickly behind the tree as Elizabeth approaches, her face a mask of concern. "What is it, Claudia?"

Claudia's eyes snap back into focus, a tremor in her voice. "Something's happened at the docks." Her gaze sharpens. "Alex!"

Elizabeth coughs and then envelopes her in a tight hug. Just then, a boy resembling the one who had been ill at Róis's—a brother perhaps, bursts from the shadows, breathless and wild-eyed. "Fuair siad corp ag na duganna!"

"A body?" Elizabeth asks the boy. "Who?"

He's too busy sprinting away to answer. Claudia stands paralyzed by the shock, her legs giving way beneath her. Elizabeth catches her just in time, preventing her collapse. Claudia shakes her head, determination replacing her terror. "We must go."

As they dash into the menacing night, a cold dread grips my heart, wrenching it down into my gut. Claudia was racing toward danger, a killer lurking in the shadows, and I was powerless to intervene. The darkness swallows me whole, suffocating, until it is all I can see.

Guarded Time

CHAPTER EIGHT – CROMWELL

"If parts allure thee, think how Bacon shined,

The wisest, brightest, meanest of mankind;

Or, ravish'd with the whistling of a name,

See Cromwell, damn'd to everlasting fame!"

Alexander Pope (1688-1744)

"They raided our supply ship," Ruarc barked, his voice echoing in the dimly lit tent. His eyes were fierce, and his hands clenched into fists at his sides. "What were we supposed to do, stand by?"

Aodhán, standing beside him with a determined expression, nodded in agreement. "Continued without relent, sir," he added, his tone sharp and unwavering. "Armed with sleánna, claidhmhe, boghanna, and sceana."

Oliver Cromwell, seated at the head of the table, leaned forward, his brow furrowed in frustration. If they had spears, swords, bows, and daggers on hand, they were certainly prepared for battle. "I understand, but you are trained soldiers," he responded, his voice low and stern. "You've decreased our advantage."

With a sudden burst of energy, Oliver pounded his fist on the wooden table, causing the maps and papers to jump. Ruarc and Aodhán stood frozen, their eyes fixed on him. Oliver took a deep breath, trying to calm the storm of thoughts swirling in his mind. "I'll have to figure out how to maintain calm while we wait for the artillery," he said, half to himself, his gaze distant.

"When should we be expecting them?" Ruarc asked, his voice laced with urgency. "I hope soon."

Oliver straightened up, his eyes meeting Ruarc's with a determined gaze. "Go speak to the men," he ordered. "Ensure they remain calm. I don't want them upset about the injured soldier."

"Yes, sir," Aodhán responded with a nod. "The lad is recovering well and should be fully mended soon."

Oliver gave a brief nod, and the two men turned on their heels, exiting the tent with a rustle of their cloaks, leaving him alone with his thoughts. He leaned back in his chair, staring at the fluttering tent flap. He had hoped to negotiate with the town, to avoid violence and keep Elizabeth safe. But Sir Arthur Aston had been obstinate, clinging stubbornly to his own terms.

As he pondered, a shadow of doubt crept over him. Had signing the death warrant for Charles I set him on a path of no return? He knew it would elevate him to Lord Protector, heralding a rise in republicanism in England, but at what cost? Could he sustain his success and protect Elizabeth, or would it all lead to his downfall and utter ruin if power was kept in his hands?

His thoughts were interrupted by the sound of hurried footsteps, and Elizabeth burst into the tent, her eyes blazing with anger. "You said there would be no bloodshed before the battle," she demanded, her voice trembling with emotion. "But a body was found at the dock!"

Oliver rose from his chair, his expression softening as he approached her. "I know, Dear," he pleaded gently. "It was against my orders. The men tell me our supply ship was raided."

Elizabeth shook her head, her lips pressed into a thin line. "That doesn't make sense. He was a good lad. And a hard worker by all reports of those employed at the dock."

"It won't happen again," Oliver promised, his voice steady and reassuring.

Elizabeth paused, her brow furrowing in thought. "Supply ship…" she murmured, a hint of worry in her voice. "So the artillery has not arrived yet?"

"No, it hasn't," Oliver admitted, reaching out to grasp her hand. "Please, Dear, do not be alarmed. I have things under control here."

Elizabeth couldn't help but roll her eyes, her expression a perfect mix of exasperation and restraint, knowing full well that a sarcastic retort would be unwise.

"How have things been going for you?" Oliver asked, smoothly steering the conversation away from potential conflict.

"Marvelous! We're even holding a ritual under the song moon," Elizabeth replied, her voice carrying a note of excitement.

"Have you asked them about the cure?" Oliver inquired, his tone shifting to one of urgency.

"I'm waiting for a moment to drop it into conversation naturally," she said, her mind already calculating the right opportunity.

"It must be found," Oliver barked, his voice ricocheting off the canvas walls of the tent, louder than he'd intended. "The curse lasts seven generations, which means it will pass to our children."

"Trust me," Elizabeth said, her voice steady but filled with understanding. "I know the urgency." She reached out to Oliver but hesitated, her hand hovering in the space between them, as if an invisible barrier—the heartbreak they'd endured—stood like a plank separating them even in their closeness.

As she exited the tent, Elizabeth paused in front of a soldier named Lochlainn. The young man was built with a robust frame, his broad shoulders rising as he noticed her presence. His uniform clung to him, outlining the muscles beneath, and his chiseled jawline softened as he met her gaze. A grin spread across his face, bringing dimples to life.

"It was awful," Lochlainn exclaimed, his voice filled with the weight of recent memories. "They caught us by surprise. We thought everyone would be at the festival."

"You did what you had to," Elizabeth said, her words gentle yet firm, offering the soldier solace that Oliver could almost feel from where he stood by the tent door, eavesdropping on their exchange.

"Elizabeth, would you do me a kindness and help me mend my britches?" another soldier called out from a short distance away, his voice breaking through the air.

"Stay your horses. I'll be right there," Elizabeth replied, her voice a blend of amusement and reassurance, as she turned to assist with the request.

"Don't let it keep you from your original mission," Elizabeth commanded Lochlainn before Oliver heard her footsteps fade into the distance.

"I'm ready for your report, Lochlainn," Oliver said, steering the man into the tent with a firm grip.

"I've spotted extra people you hadn't accounted for."

"Recruits from other towns?" Oliver's voice was sharp, expectant.

"Not quite." A deep crimson flushed between the man's freckles, even reaching his ears.

"What then?" Oliver demanded, his patience wearing thin.

"A woman new to town has joined Étaín's coven, and Étaín's son, Conor, has taken a new mate at the docks. The new mate also has a mysterious sweetheart."

Oliver's legs gave way, forcing him into a chair. "Do you know their names?" he asked, voice taut with urgency.

"No, but I can describe them."

"Spit it out already!" Oliver snapped.

"The new member of Étaín's coven has hair kissed with snow, a tender, timeless brightness in her face, and a tall, commanding presence."

Oliver inhaled sharply, the air cutting like a knife. "Keep going."

"The new dockworker is a young lad with sandy hair, a fresh look, and a mischievous smile."

Oliver's fists clenched, knuckles white with tension.

"His sweetheart is slender with dark hair and eyes that pierce straight into your soul."

"Zounds! How are they here?" Oliver's mind raced, disbelief tinged with dread.

"Sir, who are they?" Lochlainn's voice broke through Oliver's frantic thoughts.

Oliver remained silent, lost in contemplation. How was it possible that Marie, Alex, and Claudia from the 1920s were here in 1649 Ireland? He knew Marie would concoct her own scheme to thwart his plans, but he never imagined she'd be here in the flesh, and not alone.

Had his creation unleashed her ability to manipulate time and events as well? He had to apprehend them, or at the very least, keep them from obstructing his path. Claudia, the one who had driven him to create the counters, would be his primary target.

"I need you to track the young woman immediately. Her name is Claudia, though she might be using an alias," he commanded with urgency.

"Is there anything specific I should be vigilant about?" came the inquiry.

"Uncover her connections and monitor their activities—especially anything related to chants and meditation," he instructed, his voice taut with tension. As he spoke, an impenetrable wall seemed to slam into his mind. The memories of Claudia across timelines blurred, as if obscured by a thick fog. The coven was clearly at work, and he had to dismantle their influence. There was already too much on his plate with the siege and his consuming love.

"What about the young man at the docks? Could he be a spy or a new recruit for their militia?" Lochlainn pressed.

"If you're trailing Claudia, you're bound to encounter Alex," Oliver replied tersely.

"Should I be wary of anything specific with him?" Lochlainn asked.

"Nothing extraordinary when scrutinizing a man. It's the women in the trio who wield true power," Oliver retorted, his voice laced with contempt.

"How very pagan of them!" Lochlainn scoffed.

Oliver's anxiety spiked at the thought of their presence, but he reassured himself that at least they wouldn't harm

Elizabeth—they cared for her too. Yet, that didn't mean they wouldn't derail or sabotage his plans.

"Ensure the newest member of Étaín's coven, Marie, stays far away from Elizabeth," Oliver ordered, his voice edged with steel.

Lochlainn's jaw tightened at the mention of Elizabeth, and his brow furrowed with concern.

"I doubt she's using the name Marie here. I think I may have overheard others calling her Laura," Lochlainn revealed.

Understanding hit Oliver like a lightning strike—Marie needed an alias, unlike the others.

"That makes sense. Have you seen the group Elizabeth is with?" Oliver demanded, urgency crackling in his voice.

Lochlainn cleared his throat, nodding with a grave expression. "Yes, I have."

"Is Mary part of that group, and does she share any similar mannerisms with Laura?"

"That would be a little odd. Do you think they're related or something?"

"Or something would be correct." Oliver's mind raced as he pondered the bizarre circumstances that had led them to this point. Mary hadn't arrived with her old body; the original Mary was also present. Having two timelines of one soul coexisting in the same world was a dangerous game, one that he could exploit to his advantage.

If they were going to play dirty, intertwining timelines with reckless abandon, then so could he, with even greater malice.

"That will be all," Oliver commanded Lochlainn with steely resolve. "Go and join the other men outside. Ruarc and Aodhán have gathered them to receive orders."

Lochlainn snapped a sharp salute and strode out of the tent, determination etched into every step.

"Soldiers, you stand on the brink of a mission unlike any encountered before. Steel yourselves, for the path ahead will test your mettle to its very limits. Look after one another as the adrenaline courses through your veins, for this is only the beginning." Oliver's gaze swept over the troops, their heads bobbing in fierce agreement as he pressed on.

"As soon as the artillery arrives, we launch into a grueling battle. Be poised to strike the instant we breach their defenses, which might take days as no one has breached this wall before. We will unleash every weapon in our arsenal with unyielding force." He could see the fire igniting in their eyes, eager to break free from the monotony of their endless camp.

"You must be primed for combat the moment the command is given. Unforeseen challenges will arise, and we must adapt swiftly. We've devised contingency plans to outmaneuver any adversary." Their response was a cacophony of applause and shouts of fervent support. With one hand gripping his sword and the other resting on his pistol, he felt the surge of readiness that mirrored his own resolve.

Retreating to his tent, his thoughts raced. Had Marie crafted a countermeasure? What arcane forces had brought her into this fray? How would he confront this looming menace while already stretched to his limits by the siege and the need to shield his beloved? How would he finally extinguish their meddling once and for all?

CHAPTER NINE – CLAUDIA

"He would expect me to send images of Sorna and Damien falling so I opt for something else. The connection between us allows me to transform it. The new nexus will focus on collapse of his empire. Anger flares through me, bringing my heartbeat to a rapid pace." (Omitted Pieces)

My lungs burn as Elizabeth and I pound across the creaking planks of the dock. Salt-tinged wind whips at my hair, but all I can think is: Not him. Not Alex. I force myself not to imagine his life ebbing away—blood soaking his tunic, eyes dulled by death—and slam my palm to my cheek as though the sting will chase the vision out of my mind.

When we reach the end of the jetty, chaos greets us: voices rising in panicked crescendos, the scent of fear stronger than the brine. A throng of villagers clusters around something on the boards, their shoulders pressing in like storm clouds. Each second stretches taut as a bowstring, and I feel my heart splinter.

Elizabeth and I jockey for position at the crowd's edge, peering through shoulders and arms. At last, I glimpse the scuffed leather toe of a boot, the shadow of a body half-hidden beneath anxious hands. Someone slaps a pale face, attempting to coax it awake. Relief blooms—I think it isn't Alex—but then a pained scream rends the air. Heads swivel, and I follow their gaze to the right.

There stands Alex, sandy-haired and wide-eyed, next to a man doubled over in agony. My relief surges, then shatters as I see the dark stain spreading across the injured fellow's tunic. A woman kneels beside him, lifting his shirt to reveal a ragged gash that glistens wetly in the evening moonlight.

Mary bursts through the crowd, her satchel rattling. "Honey for wounds!" she calls, offering a small jar brimming with golden amber.

Barnabus appears behind her, holding a slender iron rod and a smooth knife, his expression grave. "I'll cauterize," he says, voice low. A stranger's gruff offer of whiskey passes through the throng like a lifeline.

I charge forward. Alex meets me halfway, relief flooding his features as I throw my arms around him. "Claudia," he murmurs, voice thick. We cling together amid the tumult.

A beaming young man with wind-tossed hair steps into view. "Is this your love?" he asks, extending a robust hand. "I'm Rí; we passed each other at the festival. Too loud for introductions, I'm afraid."

I press my hand into his, managing a shaky smile. Alex gestures to a broad-shouldered companion, whose dark eyes study me quietly. "This is Conor," he says. Conor inclines his head, and I realize that despite the terror of this evening, our circle has only grown tighter—and stronger—by a few more.

"She's quite beautiful," Liam remarks, glancing back at us with the whiskey bottle, now half-empty, dangling from his hand like a forgotten appendage. We exchange a tense smile with him, readying ourselves for the searing agony about to be inflicted as a hot knife is pressed to his wound to seal it shut. A harrowing scream erupts from Liam, muffled through the stick now clamped in his teeth, a primal sound of anguish that echoes in the night. His head then droops to the side, unconscious, as Mary diligently tends to the injury.

"Hugh isn't waking," Conor exclaims, drawing all eyes to the man sprawled lifelessly on the ground. A woman collapses beside him, her knees hitting the earth with a dull thud, pressing her head against his chest in a desperate plea. Her sorrow is a tangible force, heavy and raw.

Curious festival attendees, drawn by the tumult, quietly encircle the scene, placing lit candles around the prone figure until a dozen flickering flames form a solemn ring.

"What are they doing?" I ask, my voice barely above a whisper.

"Don't you know?" Rí answers, a hint of surprise in his tone. "They're warding off malevolent spirits, preventing them from claiming the soul."

"Is he dying?"

"I'm afraid so. You'll know when he's gone."

We watch as the woman beside Hugh leans close, murmuring softly into his ear. A physician crouches nearby, two fingers pressed firmly against Hugh's wrist, searching for the faintest pulse. The crowd collectively holds its breath, drawn into the gravity of the moment.

The woman, composed yet outwardly stoic, keeps her emotions in check, her focus unwavering on the physician's verdict. When he slowly shakes his head, signaling Hugh's passing, the woman's restraint shatters, and she releases a piercing howl that reverberates through us, a raw, visceral cry of grief. Those around her join in, their voices rising in a mournful chorus.

Catching sight of Elizabeth, I pull her aside. "Can't we save him? What's the use of power and magic if it can't heal?"

Elizabeth's eyes flicker across the crowd, her voice a tense whisper. "For the dead," she seethes quietly and then rubs her nose with a handkerchief. "We don't speak of it. It's forbidden."

A sudden commotion draws our attention toward Alex, a ripple of movement catching our eyes.

"They appeared out of nowhere," Conor pants, agitation in his voice. "Accused us of raiding their ship."

"We were merely securing it with mooring lines," Rí explains with a dismissive wave.

"I've never seen such a brute of a man, their leader," Liam slurs, now conscious once more. "I can't forget that freckled smile. He's the one who did this." He points shakily to the ragged gash across his chest.

Elizabeth stiffens, her posture turning rigid, as if she recognizes precisely whom Liam describes. The attackers were from Cromwell's army, a fact not entirely unexpected, yet there is an unspoken tension in her demeanor, suggesting something deeper, something more personal.

Alex gently tugs on my sleeve, his touch light yet insistent. "He's the counter I told your mother about, but she was adamant that the counters were two other guys," he whispers, his voice tinged with frustration.

"Perhaps it's best if we keep an eye on all three," I suggest softly, trying to soothe his worries. "But remember, Mother has been practicing magic for a long time and has a very trained eye," I add, hoping to reassure him.

His eyebrows knit together, a frown creasing his forehead, clearly displeased with my faith in my mother's judgment. Just then, Elizabeth tugs on my other sleeve, drawing me back into the flow of our previous conversation.

"We'll need a goose eggshell, dirt from where Hugh passed, and one of his personal belongings," Elizabeth informs me, her tone steady and purposeful.

"Where would we find a goose eggshell?" I ask, curiosity piqued.

"You can often find the birds nesting in the estuary," she replies with a knowing nod.

Barnabus and Mary approach us with a quiet shuffle. "We're going to gather food from the festival to bring to Hugh's family," Mary says, her eyes bright with determination. "You should come with us. It will make a good impression with folks."

"I'll go with you," Alex interjects, his voice firm. "In case any soldiers lie in wait."

"That would be wonderful," Barnabus responds, relief evident in his voice. "Could use another lookout."

"I need to speak with my husband about this matter," Elizabeth says, her expression serious. "I shall see you anon."

"You do that," Mary replies tersely, a hint of impatience in her tone.

As we walk toward the festival grounds, I notice Mary and Fidelma leaning into one another, their heads bowed together as if sharing secrets. Something about their closeness unsettles me, as if they're worried about something more, so I release Alex's hand and edge closer to them. Pretending to trip on a twig, I make sure to bump into Fidelma. Her face is etched with concern before shifting to shock and then understanding.

"No fair," she says, a hint of accusation in her voice. "Using the sight on me. There are rules, you know."

Sure, there are rules, but desperate times call for desperate measures. It's my turn to whisper. "They know something's amiss but haven't realized yet that there are counters here," I murmur to Alex, my voice low and urgent.

"Nor time travelers?" he murmurs softly into my good ear, his voice barely above a whisper. His eyebrows arch playfully as he continues, "You having the sight is the cat's meow."

"They plan to break Cromwell's curse!" I exclaim, the urgency in my voice barely contained.

"That would be fascinating," he muses, a hint of intrigue coloring his words. "History changing, maybe, if it works."

"Perhaps it would change his plans entirely," I suggest, pondering the possibilities.

The festival ground stands nearly deserted, the usual lively chatter replaced by a stillness as everyone has gravitated toward the docks. We take advantage of the abundance, gathering an assortment of festival food into a woven basket I clutch tightly.

"I can hold that for you," Alex offers gallantly, extending a hand.

"And how would you defend us with your hands full?" I counter with a teasing smile.

We approach Hugh's house, and his wife's face appears through the doorway, swollen and tear-streaked, unable to mask her sorrow within the privacy of her home, which we are intruding upon. She offers us gratitude through her tears, gesturing toward the kitchen table where I place the basket gently.

In the intimate confines of the kitchen, I let my eyes wander. A doll catches my attention, and a sharp pang of pain slices through me, a reminder of my own scattered timelines, where my father was often absent. Though I'm with him now, the truth of our connection remains hidden from him. The thought that this doll's owner might also face life without a father stings deeply.

Nearby, a pipe rests casually, an item I presume belonged to Hugh. Stealthily, I slip it into my pocket, aware of its necessity for the forbidden magic I must undertake. As I rejoin the others, a part of me dreads the inevitable farewell.

Once outside, Alex and I bid them a gentle goodnight. As we walk hand in hand beneath the moonlit sky, he turns to me, concern etched into his features. "We're going to see a hundred times more bloodshed if Cromwell goes through with the siege."

"Let's hope we're able to stop him," I reply, my voice laced with determination.

"Would that alter history too much?" he wonders aloud, his gaze searching mine for reassurance.

"Well, maybe we should just save Elizabeth and then travel back to our own time," I suggest, a tentative plan forming in my mind, the weight of history pressing upon us both.

"Agreed," Alex murmurs softly before his lips meet mine.

For one blissful second, a perfect, suspended moment, it feels as though we are the only two people in existence, and the rest of the world fades away into insignificance. But the weight of the pipe in my pocket abruptly pulls me back to reality. He draws me closer, his arms wrapping around me like a comforting cocoon, but I gently place a finger on his lips as they part from mine. "Speaking of Elizabeth, I need to go meet her," I whisper, my voice barely above the rustling of leaves.

"Now?" he asks, a hint of surprise in his eyes.

"Yes, it's important. Meet you at the cave?" I reply.

With a swift, tender kiss, he turns and disappears into the distance, leaving me to navigate the winding paths through the estuary. The air is thick with the scent of salt and seaweed as I carefully search for a goose eggshell, my fingers sifting through the damp earth. Finally, my efforts are rewarded, and I triumphantly return to the dock with my precious find.

There, Elizabeth is crouched low, meticulously gathering dirt from the very spot where Hugh took his last breath. Her ability to converse with Cromwell and return with such haste baffles me, but now is not the time for questions.

"You ready?" she asks, her voice steady and determined. We are about to meddle with destiny itself, and though I know I should consult my mother to understand if this is how events unfolded in the past, my resolve is unwavering. I refuse to stand by and witness another child grow up without a father if there is anything I can do to change it.

"Ready!" I declare, my voice filled with conviction.

"Morrigan, keeper of the gate, master of all fate, hear us…" Elizabeth begins, her words a solemn invocation that resonates through the air.

CHAPTER TEN – ALEXANDER

"There was nothing but crying for joy, and laughing for joy, and hugging and kissing, and when one had any time to thank the good fairy, who in the shape of a wolf, carried the child away, she was not to be found." (Fairy & Folk Tales of Ireland by W.B. Yeats)

As the salty sea breeze whipped around us, we were busy securing the ship, tying down sails and checking knots. Suddenly, a group of men emerged from the shadows, their intentions clear in their aggressive stance. At the forefront was the counter I had seen before, his presence unmistakable with an ominous aura trailing him like a dark, billowing cape. Out of the corner of my eye, I caught a glimpse of him charging toward me, his arm raised, ready to strike. My hands were tangled with the rough hemp of the ropes, leaving me no choice but to duck swiftly, feeling the rush of air as his blow narrowly missed my head.

Once I managed to free one hand and grip my scian, a small but deadly dagger, I realized the dire situation we were in. We were vastly outnumbered, and the counter wasn't alone—his partner, a burly figure with a menacing spear, flanked him. I parried the counter's sword, but his partner lunged at me, his spear thrusting forward. I sidestepped quickly, using his overextension to my advantage. As he leaned forward, off-balance, I seized the opportunity and drove my dagger into him. His scream pierced the night air, a haunting sound that jolted me awake, heart pounding and drenched in sweat.

"Are you feeling well?" Claudia's gentle voice broke through my panic, her eyes filled with concern as she sat beside me. "What is it?"

"Only a nightmare," I replied, my breaths coming in ragged gasps. Her presence was soothing, and she wrapped her arms around me, offering comfort.

"Want to talk about it?"

I hesitated, unsure if I should burden her with the vivid terror of my dream. "It was about the attack last night."

"Oh, that's awful. Did you relive it all?" she asked softly, brushing her fingers through my hair in a calming rhythm.

"Sword fights are much different than gun fights," I murmured, the memory still fresh and raw. "With a gun, you can shoot a man from a distance. With a dagger, you're close enough to see his eyes as you push metal through his flesh."

"That sounds horrible. I'm sorry you had to go through that," she whispered, pulling me closer. Her warmth was a balm to my frayed nerves.

"I'm glad you weren't there to witness it," I said, grateful for her safety as she embraced me again.

"I did notice something right before you left the festival," Claudia mentioned, a thoughtful frown on her face.

"Oh, no! Something happened there too?" I asked, a new wave of worry washing over me.

"Nothing like that. It's only that I saw you cover your ears before the horn sounded…there wasn't any noise…or at least I didn't see anyone else react."

"There was a loud ringing in my ears, but only for a second. Not like your constant ringing," I explained, recalling the brief, jarring sound.

"I think we should test your hearing. That could be a sign of hearing loss," she suggested, her tone gentle yet firm.

I was at a loss for words. The prospect of losing my hearing right before a potential battle was daunting. Given who I was speaking with, I was cautious not to react negatively.

"How do we go about testing my hearing?" I probed.

"We lack an audiometer here in 1649, and the tuning fork hasn't been invented yet," she replied.

"I haven't observed any changes in my hearing other than the ringing," I noted.

She dashed to Marie's basket, retrieving a spoon and fork. Returning swiftly, she guided me to the center of the open space.

"Close your eyes. Raise your hand when you hear this sound," she instructed, clanging the spoon and fork together as she moved around. I dutifully raised my hand each time.

She continued the clanging at intervals, and I responded each time. "Good, your hearing volume seems to align with my good ear," she concluded.

Her assessment brought a wave of relief.

"Now I'll conduct a few more rounds to determine if other pitches are similarly perceived," she announced.

It was reassuring to distinguish the different pitches she generated. Then, I felt her hand gently rest on my forearm and opened my eyes.

"You have some hearing loss, particularly with high pitches," she revealed.

"Really?" I inquired, seeking confirmation.

"It might be due to your work at the warehouses and the dock. It's quite common," she explained.

"Could this account for the sudden, overwhelming ringing I've been experiencing lately?" I questioned further.

"Have you ever experienced ringing in your ears before?" she asked, delving deeper.

"No, never," I responded, pondering the implications of her findings.

"This alteration in hearing seems to have gradually developed over time, yet the ringing is abrupt and intense," she observed, tapping her chin thoughtfully as she mulled over the phenomenon I was experiencing. Her contemplative demeanor reminded me of how she could discern Fidelma's thoughts merely by touching her.

"You've acquired a new ability," I noted to Claudia.

"You're correct, it appears I have," she acknowledged.

"Being able to understand others' thoughts could be advantageous. But what purpose does the ringing in my head serve?"

"It could be a harbinger of sorts. Like maybe it was alerting you to the oncoming attack."

"Wait, attack me! I want to see if I hear ringing."

"I doubt it functions that way. It likely requires an attack from someone with harmful intentions," she reasoned.

"What insights have you gained about your new ability?" I inquired, probing further.

"Elizabeth believes it began here because I'm somehow connected to this place."

"But she doesn't know, right?"

"I don't know how she would. I would like to test something though."

She must have seen the shadow of disappointment flit across my face, as I had grown weary of endless tests. Claudia wrapped her arms around my neck, pulling me closer with a tender determination.

"Just as I thought, no sight. My new power is confined to the souls that belong to this time," she explained, a hint of regret in her voice.

"So you can't read my thoughts right now?" I asked, drawing her in until our bodies melded. My fingers wove through her hair as if drawn by an invisible force, like magnets irresistibly pulling us together. One hand settled at her hip while the other caressed the nape of her neck, and I pressed my lips softly below her ear.

"Oh, I can read your thoughts, but not because of the sight. Maybe we should test it more," she murmured before capturing my mouth with hers. Our lips fused, and her hands gripped my arms with a fervent intensity. Her tongue danced with mine, igniting a fire deep in my belly, my muscles tightening in response.

Our chins moved in a harmonious rhythm as we fell deeper into the kiss. Claudia's breathing grew uneven, a testament to the fervor between us. We stumbled toward our sleeping spot, unable to keep our hands from exploring each other. She deftly removed my tunic, her fingers blazing trails of heat across my skin. I fumbled with the laces on her chest, urgency in every tug, desperate to press my lips to every inch of her.

"You're beautiful," I breathed as our clothes fell away. My hand traveled past her lower stomach, feeling the inviting warmth, and I massaged gently. She arched her back in response, her eyes dark and fully dilated, and I could no longer restrain myself. Propping myself on my elbows, I hovered above her, our bodies a seamless union as I kissed her deeply.

Her grip on my shoulders was fierce as I entered her, driving us both to a state of wild abandon. Our movements echoed a primordial rhythm, each one building in intensity. It was an ecstasy unlike anything I had ever experienced, our bodies gliding in perfect harmony. Claudia whispered my name as we reached the crescendo, teetering on the brink. As she surrendered to the peak, so did I, tumbling over the edge together.

Breathless, I gently disentangled our bodies to lie beside her, gazing at her exquisite face. A curious expression played across her features, as if a new thought had taken root. "What is it?" I asked, placing a soft kiss on her cheek.

"I'm recollecting the peculiar timeline, like an echo of another reality, spawned due to Cromwell's maneuvers."

"Not entirely sure that one rings a bell."

"In that reality, I had a certain clairvoyance, or rather, my spirit did, allowing me to perceive even your essence with a mere touch."

"Curious why that's not possible here."

"Honestly, I'm relieved it's not. It kept us at a distance back then."

"Yeah, definitely better this way."

She playfully kissed my nose, responding to my musings with a smile. "In that timeline, my friend heard a ringing in her ears."

"What implications did that hold for her?"

"It signified the presence of death nearby."

"That's unsettling."

"It might not be the same in this iteration. Perhaps we should investigate further?"

"If it means more tests, I'd prefer an imaginative approach."
I raised my eyebrows suggestively, prompting a gentle slap on
my arm and Claudia's radiant grin.

"I hypothesize that my lack of sight with you is due to your
time-traveling nature, but that warrants testing as well."

"Yes, Doctor, what are your instructions?" She squealed
with delight and nestled into me.

I gently traced circles on her earlobe until she peacefully
drifted into slumber. As I observed her, my mind wandered
back to Elizabeth's suggestion that Claudia's powers might
indicate a connection to this place. But what if it's a link to this
location in a broader sense?

Envisioning faeries and their tranquil havens nestled within
this verdant land, I gently drifted back into the embrace of
slumber. The dream descended upon me swiftly and vividly. At
the heart of an ancient stone circle, a disembodied voice
resonated through the air. "Remember the wisdom of the
female philosophers," it intoned with an ethereal clarity. I cast
my gaze around, seeking the dream's enigmatic source, yet it
eluded me, hidden in the mists of my subconscious.

Why had our world transitioned from the nurturing embrace
of female leadership, rich with empathy and understanding, to
a dominion of male authority, driven by an insatiable hunger
for power? In the vibrant 1920s, I had longed for my mother to
wield more influence over our family's financial matters. But

now, here in the year 1649, I stood witness to the very shift of leadership paradigms unraveling before my eyes.

My thoughts spiraled back to the tantalizing possibility of averting a siege here, and how such a change might alter the course of Ireland's history, potentially halting its colonization. What ripples could that send through time? Would it empower my mother with greater financial agency, or could it unleash unforeseen and calamitous consequences?

Our mission was clear: to ensure Elizabeth's safety and to prevent the creation of additional counters. If three counters existed in this 17th-century timeline, rather than the anticipated two, could a third have emerged from the machinations of someone other than Cromwell? What significance would this hold, and how might it reshape our future?

Claudia and I both stirred from our slumber, a clanking noise beneath the "skylight" suggesting Marie's presence. Claudia nestled closer against me, her warmth a comforting presence. I made a silent vow to myself, resolute in my determination to unravel this intricate mystery and to protect the radiant woman before me, whom I cherished with every fiber of my being.

CHAPTER ELEVEN – MARIE

Hansen - 121

"Last night turned very sad after you left," Onóra informs me, her eyes heavy with the weight of unshed tears.

"I've heard," I reply, my voice tinged with sorrow. "Tragic about Hugh. Is Liam going to be all right?"

"Yes," Róis interjects, her hands clasped tightly together. "Barnabus cauterized his wound with a steady hand, and Mary applied a soothing ointment that smelled of lavender and thyme. A lost soul is devastating, but at least one was saved."

Guilt engulfs me, a dark cloud that settles deep in my chest, as I think about all the souls that will be lost to the siege. It's like a burn that throbs and never ceases, a reminder of the lives hanging in the balance. Could I reincarnate Hugh, or would that cause a rip in the fabric of time, an irreversible tear in the delicate weave of destiny?

"I say we bind the bastards from doing any more harm," Étaín proclaims, her voice sharp with anger. "My boy was part of the group they attacked."

"Where are your quill, ink, and paper?" I ask Róis, eager to set our plans in motion.

"Oh, and ribbon?" Neasa adds, her eyes bright with determination.

Róis rummages through a wooden chest, extracting most of the items, but she's missing ink. "We'll need to run to the mercantile for ink," she admits, glancing around the dimly lit room.

I hope she doesn't want us all to go, as it would be likely we could run into Barnabus and Mary, myself from a past life—this past life. The thought sends a shiver down my spine.

"My ankle still hurts from last night," Étaín says, rubbing it gingerly.

"Well, no wonder," Róis replies, a hint of admiration in her voice. "You ran faster than lightning to see if Conor was okay, pushing through the chaos with sheer determination."

"You should have seen it, Laura," Neasa tells me, her eyes wide with the memory of the night's events.

"Why don't you stay here and let your ankle rest?" I suggest gently. "I can remain as well to keep you company."

"Okay, okay," Étaín barks, though her voice softens a touch. "It's only an ankle. Calm down."

Watching Onóra, Neasa, and Róis go, another pang hits me in the chest, a sharp reminder of the bonds I had neglected. Why had I not been closer to them in my past life? Their presence now feels like a lifeline, threads of connection I couldn't imagine going through the current circumstance without.

Feeling eyes on me, I turn to Étaín, who is studying me intently.

"Uh, huh," she huffs, suspicion lurking beneath her words. "I knew there was something off about you. Where was it you said you're from?"

"Well, I've been in America, but I'm originally from Ireland," I reply, trying to keep my tone steady.

"Yeah, but where in Ireland?" she interrogates, her gaze unwavering. "Because you watched those three leave as if you've known them your entire life."

"But doesn't it feel like it's been a lifetime since we've met, with the shadow of battle looming over us, the vibrant colors of the festival, and then the sting of heartache?" Her eyes search mine, and I worry she'll probe deeper into the question I've sidestepped.

"That festival was spectacular, wasn't it?" she says, her face lighting up as she recalls the event. Her cheeks flush with the memory.

"Sure was," I reply, relieved at the change in topic. "You even joined the dance for a song. You're a remarkable dancer." I remember how she twirled, her dress flaring like a kaleidoscope.

"Oh, go shoe the goose," she retorts with a playful grin. "I'm no dancer, but only a festival can make me feel light enough to try."

"Yeah, I can see that. It's too bad it had to be interrupted and end early." The laughter from the festival still echoes in my mind, now replaced by tension.

"All because of those nincompoops not understanding what dockworkers do and attacking them while they were doing their job," she says, her voice tinged with frustration.

"Nincompoops for sure," I agree, and we both break into laughter, the kind that shakes your shoulders and eases tension for a moment.

"But why was the boat on our side instead of their camp side?" I ask, a frown creasing my brow.

Étaín suddenly sits up straight, eyes wide. "You're right!"

"It was just a question. You going somewhere?" I ask as she begins to rise.

"They may have planted something at the harbor. I need to warn my boy," she says with urgency, her words quickening.

"Hang on." I gently place my hand on her arm. "Maybe they are just nincompoops and made an error."

"That's true, but something still feels off about it." She takes a step forward, her face tightening in pain as she winces.

"Be careful. You need to let your ankle heal," I remind her, concern lacing my voice.

She reluctantly sits down, crossing her arms with a sigh, her mind clearly racing.

"Surely if they'd planted weapons, Conor would have noticed. He's sharp like his mother."

Étaín graces me with her brilliant lopsided smile with that note.

"Do you know whose names we'll write down?" I ask her.

"Well, Cromwell, for sure. Conor thought he overheard one of the attackers call their leader Lochlainn."

I ponder on this for a bit. Cromwell makes sense, though he isn't usually the one who physically causes harm. Instead, he orders someone else to do it on his behalf. Could this Lochlainn fellow be one of the counters? I'm not sure, but something else hits me.

"Isn't Lochlainn an Irish name, not an English one?"

"Yeah, you're right. A traitor and an arsehole, he is."

As I think on this information and what it could mean, Róis, Neasa, and Onóra return holding a couple of bottles of ink.

"Ready?" Onóra asks.

We gather around the table, placing the inventory of items in order: quill, ink, paper, and ribbon. A small thrum of excitement moves through me in anticipation.

Neasa writes Cromwell's name on a paper while Étaín writes Lochlainn's on another.

"Will that be enough?" Róis asks.

"Do you know any more of their names?" Étaín retorts.

Róis shrugs while I roll the papers and hand them to Onóra and Róis, one each. As they tie the ribbon around them in the knots, we recite:

"Bind this tight, hold it fast,

Mind our words, make it last.

Let no harm come to our town,

For good of all so mote it be."

I visualize peace and no siege, picturing Cromwell and his army leaving Drogheda. Then we go outside to bury the papers where they won't be disturbed, but we're interrupted.

"I heard you," an Englishman outside Róis's home says. "You're all a bunch of witches. I'm going to report you."

Movement catches my peripheral. Étaín isn't standing around to see what the man does next. Is she running? Then, whack, she thumps him on the head with a skillet, and he falls.

"Étaín, we could be charged with assault!" Neasa exclaims.

"Punishment for that wouldn't be any worse than for witchcraft." Onóra shrugs.

"Do you have a wheelbarrow or something?" I ask.

"Why?" Róis squeaks. "To move him, where?"

"Yeah, take him to the pub," Étaín says, liking my idea. "Pour a beer on him so all the patrons convince him he's lost his mind if he wakes up talking about us." I notice she's putting all her weight on the good ankle as she possibly hurt her other one while whacking him on the head.

Conor and Rí walk up just then. "Ma, what did you do? He's in a complete stupor."

"What makes you think it was me?" Étaín asks. "There are four other ladies here."

"Ma? You're right, but they are ladies and you're…"

She smacks him upside the head before he can finish. He notices her wince when she steps with her bad ankle.

"You all right?" he asks as he assists her to a chair.

"Fine, just need to figure out how to move this man to the pub and cover him with beer so people think he's crazy when he goes around calling us witches."

"Ma! What were you…"

He's again brought to silence but this time with only a look.

"Go get the wheelbarrow so you can move him," Étaín orders.

Without further argument, Conor and Rí are off to their task, and the women all bid farewell too as we leave Róis's dwelling. Apparently, the activity has been enough for everyone. Rí looks like a lost pup as the boys go away. Onóra has one of Étaín's arms over her shoulders while Neasa has the other as they help her leave.

Instead of heading to the cave, I turn toward the drawbridge. Something's not right. We've barely found any information on the counters. If one of them was part of the attack, it doesn't make sense that he'd be Irish. Knowing my sister, Claudia's having a difficult time keeping her out of the fray.

I must spy on Cromwell myself, once and for all, to finally put an end to this madness. Determined, I stop in town to procure a dark hooded cloak, feeling a surge of confidence with my newfound anonymity. The fabric caresses my cheeks like a secret whisper as I drape it over my shoulders. I justify the expense, knowing the impending chill and planning to share it with Claudia.

As I near the drawbridge, I observe the usual throng. Drogheda's citizens would slip through the wall gates with ease, unlike the soldiers, who would need to disguise themselves as fishermen or bartenders to blend in. Workers trudge homeward, moving against my path over the drawbridge. Children dart and play in the fading light. A few passersby are cloaked like me, and I feel a gratifying sense of belonging amidst the shadows.

I strain my eyes toward the camp, hoping to see or hear something from the wall, though I suspect I'll need to venture closer. I'll cross that bridge when I come to it, pun intended.

A shadow looms across my path. As I glance up, the face beneath the hood remains obscured. I sidestep to the left, but they mimic my movement. I veer right, and our awkward dance continues in tense silence.

Without warning, the figure seizes my arm, yanking me into the depths of their cloak. A hand clamps over my mouth, stifling my scream. A voice, gruff and chilling, murmurs close to my ear, sending shivers down my spine. "Well, well, look who we have here," Oliver Cromwell's gravelly whisper resurrects every haunting memory of his past atrocities.

I thrash, desperate to break free, but his grip tightens like a vice. He signals to a couple of his men, and before I can bite him, a gag is forced into my mouth. A woman with a young child witnesses this, fleeing in terror. The men seize my arms, dragging me relentlessly to the edge of the drawbridge.

They bind me with a rope, and I am lowered over the side toward a waiting boat. Panic surges as I contemplate my fate—whether they're taking me to the camp or to my death. My heartbeat thunders in my ears, drowning out all thoughts as adrenaline courses through my veins.

CHAPTER TWELVE – CROMWELL

"This is a righteous judgement of God upon these barbarous wretches, who have imbrued their hands in so much innocent blood...."

Oliver Cromwell after the storming of Drogheda. 1649.

"What are you doing here, Marie?" Oliver Cromwell asked, his penetrating gaze fixed on his captive. The dim light of the tent cast long shadows across his face, highlighting his stern expression.

Ruarc interjected before Marie, or rather Laura, could respond. "If you and your daughter won't stop interfering, we will stop you." His voice was sharp, echoing the tension within the enclosed space.

"Very brave, Child, but you wouldn't even exist if it weren't for me, at least your soul as you know it now," Marie retorted, her words laced with a mixture of defiance and wit.

"I'm no child, and you had no part in my existence," Ruarc barked, his tone brimming with indignation.

Oliver shrugged nonchalantly. "That's not entirely true." His words hung in the air like a suspenseful note, causing Ruarc and Aodhán to exchange anxious glances.

"What does that mean?" Aodhán inquired, his eyes wide with shock. Both he and Ruarc shifted uneasily, their agitation palpable.

"How 'bout you two give us some privacy," Oliver commanded his men. Though confusion flickered across their faces, they obeyed the order, leaving the tent and allowing the flap to fall closed behind them.

"I have to say," Marie addressed Oliver, her voice steady, "they're loyal." Her gaze followed the soldiers' retreating forms.

"Did you expect anything different from a decorated military leader?" Oliver replied, pacing back and forth. His strides were purposeful, each step sending small clouds of dust swirling up from the earthen floor.

"How did you time travel? It must have been magic. Don't think I can't tell you've been using it on me!" His voice rose, tinged with accusation, as he halted abruptly to face her.

"Excuse me," Marie said, shifting her bound wrists with a jingle of chains. "What makes you think I'd tell you how to do anything?"

"Your coven bound me." Oliver slammed his fists down on the wooden table, causing it to rattle. "You didn't think I wouldn't notice the dream invasion?"

A smirk flitted across Marie's lips, but it vanished swiftly as Oliver mirrored her expression. Her brow furrowed in puzzlement at his unexpected composure. Sniffing the air, her eyes roamed the tent, eventually settling on candles adorned with bay leaves protruding from glass jars.

"You didn't think Elizabeth would keep magical knowledge from me, did you?" Oliver's smirk widened, a glint of triumph in his eyes.

"Is that how you were able to create the counters?" Marie asked, her voice tinged with curiosity and suspicion.

"It took me a lot longer to master magic with no coven, so once I did, I made a coven of my own."

"Those entities are no coven. What are they?" Marie's brow knitted in confusion as she attempted to piece together the puzzle on her own, her thoughts racing through the possibilities.

"After all this time, I'd have thought you would have paid closer attention to me," Oliver remarked with a pout that was meant to mock Marie rather than convey genuine hurt. His expression was a mask of indifference; the situation had worked to his advantage, after all.

Marie, regaining her composure after the initial shock, retorted, "You've always thought so highly of yourself, haven't you?" Her voice was steady, with a hint of disdain.

Oliver leaned back, a self-satisfied smirk playing on his lips. "I did figure out how to alter DNA long before the rest of the world did, didn't I?" His words were laced with arrogance.

Marie crossed her arms, her eyes narrowing. "Pretty easy when you hold the knowledge of all your timelines," she replied, her tone cutting.

"Perhaps," Oliver conceded, "but I also created clones, non-bio copies, and even total transplantation." His voice was filled with a pride that resonated with each syllable.

"You never knew when to call it quits, just like with the siege. Civilians, you had no mercy," Marie accused, her voice rising slightly as she recalled the past.

Oliver's face darkened, shadows playing over his features. "And you know exactly what caused me to go through such extreme measures that time!" he shot back, his voice edged with bitterness.

"So, you're not going to do that this time?" Marie asked, her voice softening slightly, a touch of hope lacing her words.

"Not if you finally allow me to save Elizabeth and stop your incessant interfering," Oliver replied, his tone firm and unwavering.

"Is that how you see it? Not that your crossing lines and boundaries has always been the cause of your suffering?" Marie countered, her voice a blend of exasperation and understanding.

Oliver, his patience wearing thin, raised his voice. "At least I was smart enough not to have two bodies of the same soul in the same timeline."

Marie's voice was tempered, almost amused, as she responded, "Noticed that, did you?"

"It would be rather bad if Mary—old you—ran into you here, wouldn't it?" Oliver pointed out, his eyes narrowing slightly.

"And you've what? Brought past and future souls into the same body! How did you even manage that?" Marie asked, her curiosity tinged with disbelief.

Oliver's lips curled into a smile, his eyes glinting with mischief. "Oh, I have many talents, and I'm not the only one!" His voice carried a hint of mystery, leaving his statement hanging in the air between them. "Ruarc and Aodhán have always been my closest allies."

"How does it feel? Are there any ill effects?" Marie's voice was laced with curiosity, her eyes probing Oliver intensely.

"Only you could bring such an accomplishment down," Oliver replied, his tone a blend of frustration and admiration, as he paced back and forth across the dimly lit tent.

"So there are negative results then," Marie pressed, a slow wave of contentment spreading through her body like a warm tide. The air around them was tense, thick with unspoken truths and the smell of damp earth.

"It's nothing that can't be managed," Oliver retorted, his voice steady but his eyes flickering with unease, betraying the tension beneath his calm exterior.

"There's an odd feeling to it, isn't there?" Marie continued, her voice a soft whisper, almost as if she was speaking to herself.

"What do you know?" Oliver snapped, his patience wearing thin as he stopped abruptly, his eyes narrowing at her.

"And you haven't even warned them?" Marie asked, her eyebrow arching sharply in skepticism. "Just expect them to obey your command."

"Enough of this," Oliver's voice rose with authority, cutting through the thick atmosphere like a knife. He turned sharply on his heel and ordered his men, who stood at attention, to return. "Be sure she's secure!"

Aodhán, a tall figure with a rugged demeanor, approached Marie with a critical eye, checking her chains with a practiced hand. The clinking of metal echoed softly as he ensured the stake driven firmly into the ground was unyielding. "All good," he said, his voice gruff yet reassuring to Oliver.

"What next?" Ruarc asked, his eyes glinting with a mixture of anticipation and readiness. "The men are ready. Are we to join the battle?"

"You're still going through with it?" Marie yanked against her chains, her voice rising with a mix of disbelief and desperation.

"Hush," Oliver snapped, his words sharp as he turned to his two closest allies. "Get her daughter, Claudia, and then you can join the battle."

"No, you wouldn't," Marie yelled, her voice breaking with emotion. "Haven't you messed with her enough? And where has it gotten you?" Her voice lingered in the air, a haunting melody of defiance and despair.

With a brutal strike, Oliver silenced Marie with the butt of his pistol. The impact on the side of her head rendered her unconscious instantly, finally bringing the silence he craved. He would crack the secret of her clone counter when he had her daughter in his grasp as leverage.

Oliver stormed out of the tent, eyes fixed on the transport ships and his cannon edging into position on the Boyne River. He barked orders to his men, commanding them to haul the massive artillery pieces into strategic positions—some set on the slopes dominating the town, others in the lower grounds ready to assault the walls.

His heart swelled with a fierce pride as he watched his men operate with machine-like precision. It was a spectacle of military pageantry, their rigid, formal formation a testament to their training. They moved as one, a perfectly synchronized force.

The memories flooded back, pulling him to that pivotal first moment. Back then, he had not foreseen losing Elizabeth. Now, thanks to Marie's meddling, her fate once again hung uncertainly in the balance.

As he gazed at the formidable Drogheda walls, a surge of panic clawed up his throat. Would the cannon's might suffice? He reassured himself with the bitter knowledge that it had been enough once before. Surely, it would prevail again.

But then, a mist began to coil its way toward him, swirling ominously over the water. There was no rational explanation— the cannons were silent, the weather unchanged. A chilling realization struck him: it was supernatural. Elizabeth had once spoken of this—a veil between the human realm and the Otherworld.

Within this mist, magical beings roamed unfettered. Only one thing could have triggered such an anomaly. It was unfortunate he needed Marie alive to ensure his own reincarnation. He reasoned that forcing Marie to act might avert future disasters. By eliminating Elizabeth's threat, Mary would have no cause to reincarnate, thus halting Barnabus and Claudia as well. He could compel Marie—or Laura—to reincarnate Elizabeth so he could love her for eternity, finally and irrevocably.

But first, he needed to halt Marie from conjuring this enigmatic mist, however she was managing it. How had she regained consciousness so quickly? Determined, he stormed back to his tent, aware that the men still had hours of tasks to complete. He pushed through the tent flap with a sense of urgency, but Marie appeared as if she had been expecting him, her composed demeanor aggravating him even further.

"You know, you've made huge mistakes in every timeline," he declared, his voice edged with frustration.

"Oh, yeah? Do tell?" she replied, her calmness unnerving him as he struggled to understand her serene facade.

"Claudia—well, I suppose she was Austria in the haunted house timeline—had only been away from your home for a few months before her life was in peril. Great parenting skills!" he retorted, his sarcasm cutting through the air like a knife.

"Oh, you should be talking. You lost a child long before mine was ever in danger," she shot back, her words stinging with unexpected venom.

"That's low, even for you," he snapped, a flicker of anger crossing his face.

"What do you expect when you have those two going after my daughter!" she countered, her voice rising in intensity.

"Then in the timeline with multiple planets, she ran away from you!" Oliver continued, his persistence fueled by the knowledge that Marie's rare outburst indicated he was striking a nerve, and he intended to keep pressing.

"Yeah, because she had to go save her dad from you!" she exclaimed, her words laced with a mixture of frustration and defiance.

"How is Barnabus anyway? Oh wait, you can't see him, can you? That's got to be hard!" he taunted, his words dripping with mock sympathy.

Marie let out an exasperated groan, her patience wearing thin. "Are you getting to the point?" she demanded, her voice tinged with irritation.

"You weren't even present in the ghostly counterworld, and you lost Elizabeth—Anne in the Prohibition timeline. How do you think you can possibly save her now?" he challenged, his words hanging in the air like a dark cloud.

"I'm assuming you have a foolproof plan to save her then. How's that going?" she retorted, her skepticism evident.

"It would be fine if you weren't here," he replied, his frustration palpable in the tense atmosphere.

A soldier entered the dimly lit tent, his boots thudding against the dirt floor, and handed Oliver a stack of crisp parchment, a quill, and a small pot of ink. With a determined furrow in his brow, Oliver sat at the wooden table, the flickering candle casting shadows over his face, and began to pen a letter. His hope was pinned on this message, that Sir Arthur Aston would finally see reason and agree to surrender.

The note was concise yet firm, each word carefully chosen, but Oliver meticulously blew on the damp ink, ensuring it dried perfectly to avoid smudging as he folded the paper. He dripped hot wax onto the seal, pressing it with his signet ring, ensuring the message remained untouched until it reached its intended reader.

The soldier, standing at attention, took the sealed note and marched briskly out of the tent, the flap rustling behind him.

"Do you think Sir Aston will actually listen to you this time?" Marie asked, arms crossed, her tone laced with doubt. "You should have waited until you made more headway on the wall since it will take days to break through."

"I've never wanted to damage this city, Elizabeth's home!" Oliver retorted, his voice rising with the fervor of his conviction.

"Right, like I believe that," Marie scoffed, rolling her eyes.

"I have a message for you too," Oliver said, his voice steadying.

"Great!" Marie exclaimed with exaggerated enthusiasm, her sarcasm cutting through the air.

"Reincarnate only Elizabeth and myself," Oliver instructed, his eyes locking onto hers with an intensity that demanded attention.

"And why would I do that?" Marie questioned, her eyes narrowing in suspicion.

"Because it will keep Claudia safe," Oliver replied, the earnestness in his voice momentarily softening the tension between them.

Marie hesitated, a flicker of uncertainty crossing her face as she processed his words. Emotions battled across her features until she settled on a defiant stance.

"If I don't reincarnate myself and Barnabus, the Claudia you're having brought here won't exist. There goes your leverage," she rebutted, her words striking Oliver like a cold splash of reality.

That seemed to silence him for a moment. His plans had revolved so intensely around Elizabeth that he hadn't considered this angle.

"Well, it's your choice. Either she dies a painful death or softly floats out of existence," Oliver stated, his voice tinged with a grim finality.

He huffed, frustration bubbling over as he stormed out of the tent. His mind raced, realizing that in his eagerness to secure reincarnation for himself and Elizabeth, he had inadvertently revealed too much too soon. Now he faced the daunting task of uncovering who was behind the third counter.

Determined to regroup, he headed to another tent, unwilling to spend another moment under the same canvas as Marie. As he settled onto a cot, he began to devise a new strategy, his mind whirring with possibilities during the quiet hours of the night.

CHAPTER THIRTEEN – CLAUDIA

"The English may batter us to pieces, but they will never succeed in breaking our spirit."

Maud Gonne

Barnabus collects logs meticulously prepared from large oak branches that had been scattered by a fierce storm. Elizabeth and I venture into the woods, our eyes scanning for dry twigs and small branches to use as kindling. The early morning chill bites at my skin, and the silvery light of the moon seems to distort my senses. Meanwhile, Fidelma, Líadan, and Mary gather pitchers of water, clay cups, and an assortment of snacks. Our designated meeting spot is the ancient hawthorn tree, its gnarled branches silhouetted against the night sky.

As the fire crackles and grows, we form a circle, warmth radiating from the flames. They stretch their arms wide, and I mimic their fluid movements. Each person then begins to move freely, expressing themselves in their own way. I let my instincts guide me—arms extended, I bend them at the elbows, hands directed downward. Slowly, I twist them back toward my body until they stretch out wide again, palms open to the sky.

A sense of lightness fills me. We exchange glances, a silent understanding passing between us. Barnabus speaks first, his voice steady, "I wish to send strength to the young men facing the battalion."

Mary follows, her tone firm. "I wish for the wall to hold steady against the enemy."

Fidelma's eyes gleam with determination as she adds, "I wish to be able to return to Brehon Law, which allowed me to love whomever I desired." She shares a knowing smile with Líadan.

"May the Tuatha Dé Danann reign fury upon the Sasanachs," Líadan proclaims, her voice carrying a fierce resolve.

A gentle vibration hums through the air, resonating with an indescribable energy. We gaze upwards, captivated by the tapestry of stars twinkling above. The towering trees surrounding us rustle their leaves, whispering secrets in the moonlight, while the lush green earth beneath us glows with an ethereal beauty.

Barnabus raises his voice, invoking ancient names, "We call on Tarbh, Cú, Scorpion, and An tUisceadóir."

Kneeling side by side, we place our arms on each other's shoulders, swaying together in a unified rhythm. I silently hope our wishes find their way to fulfillment.

Mary turns to Elizabeth, curiosity piqued. "Did you not have a wish?" she asks gently.

Elizabeth fidgets, entwining her fingers nervously. "I don't think you'll like it," she admits, her voice tinged with hesitation.

"Is it important to you?" Mary presses.

"Yes, it protects my children!" Elizabeth asserts, her eyes filled with a fierce maternal determination.

"What is it?" Mary inquires, her interest genuine.

"I want to break the curse on my husband. It will require us to move to a different location, but I believe it might be enough to stop his attack as well!" Elizabeth reveals, her voice a blend of hope and desperation.

Mary considers her sister's words, her expression softening. "Not that Oliver deserves any help from us, but I'll do it for you," she agrees, conceding to her sister's heartfelt plea.

"Where do we need to go, and how far is it?" Barnabus inquires, his voice tinged with curiosity and a hint of urgency. His brow furrows slightly as he awaits the answer.

"We need to go to Brú na Bóinne," Elizabeth replies, her eyes scanning the horizon as if already envisioning the journey ahead. "It's about an hour on horseback. I've brought horses." Her tone is confident, as if she's already planned every step of the way.

"There's so much to prepare for," Fidelma interjects, her voice sharp with concern. She crosses her arms tightly across her chest. "Do you really think it could stop the attack?"

"And where did you get horses from?" Líadan adds, her eyes narrowing in suspicion.

"They may or may not belong to the enemy's cavalry," Elizabeth responds, a slow, sly smile creeping over her lips, her eyes glinting with mischief.

"Guess that's another way to stop the fighting," I exclaim, raising an eyebrow in admiration and disbelief. "How did you manage to get them out unnoticed?"

Elizabeth shrugs, a casualness in her demeanor that belies the audacity of her actions. "The men might be under my husband's command, but many listen to me."

Fidelma taps her fingers together, her eyes alight with a conspiratorial gleam as if she's already plotting the next move.

As we walk to where Elizabeth has hidden the horses, my stomach churns with nervousness. Will they be able to tell I've only ridden a horse a handful of times? My childhood memories are filled with the gentle sway of carriages and the rumble of cars from more recent years, not the unpredictable gait of a horse.

"What is this thing?" Barnabus asks, pointing to the leather contraption strapped to a horse's back, his finger hovering as if afraid to touch it.

"It's a saddle," Elizabeth explains patiently, patting the smooth leather with familiarity. "The English use them to help ride because not only does it help the rider's balance but also the horse's comfort."

"If you say so," Barnabus mutters, skepticism woven into his words as he takes a step back, eyeing the saddle with distrust.

Perhaps I won't be the only one out of my element. At least, the few times I'd ridden a horse, it had been with a saddle.

During the ride, the saddle creaks beneath me as I sway from side to side, trying to find my balance. My fingers grip the leather reins awkwardly at first, but soon I settle into a steady rhythm. Fortunately, my horse seems quite content to trail behind the others, its hooves lightly thudding against the ground, requiring little guidance from me. In contrast, Barnabus appears uneasy, shifting his weight nervously on his saddle. When Elizabeth suddenly erupts into a coughing fit, Barnabus wobbles precariously, nearly toppling over.

As we approach a towering grassy mound encircled by an ancient stone wall, our pace instinctively slows. My eyes widen with wonder, and Elizabeth notices. "Welcome to Brú na Bóinne," she says, smiling at my evident awe. The mound seems to stretch across an entire acre, its presence both imposing and mesmerizing. As I walk toward the entrance, my gaze is drawn to intricate engravings etched into the stone, each line and curve telling a silent story. Inside, the space is even more captivating, the walls adorned with engraved stones that lend an otherworldly atmosphere.

"This structure was built over four millennia ago," Elizabeth explains, her voice echoing softly against the stone. "The nineteen-meter passageway leads to the chamber we're headed to. It's aligned with the rising sun."

"It's amazing!" I manage to say, my voice barely above a whisper, overwhelmed by the sheer magnitude of history surrounding us.

"So, what are we going to do now that we're here?" Fidelma asks, her curiosity piqued.

Elizabeth reaches into her satchel and pulls out a smooth stone, its surface glistening with a faint sheen. "I have a stone from the river where I bathed my child before the burial," she says, handing the stone to Mary, who cradles it gently in her hands.

"I also have a stone from the river where Oliver bathed as a child," Elizabeth adds, glancing at Líadan with a questioning look.

"Don't look at me," Líadan protests, raising her hands defensively. "I'm not touching that thing."

Elizabeth rolls her eyes with a sigh, then passes the stone to Barnabus. She hands Fidelma and Líadan each a horseshoe. "Don't worry. These have only been touched by the blacksmith and myself," she assures them.

Finally, she approaches me, holding out a delicate gold necklace. "This belonged to another Elizabeth. Miss Wyckes married Oliver's great, great uncle, Thomas," she explains, her eyes reflecting the necklace's rich history.

She hands me the necklace, its chain cool and smooth against my palm, and suddenly a vivid vision engulfs me. In the scene, a woman, perhaps only a few years younger than my mother, lies on a bed. Her skin glistens with sweat, and each cough rasps through her body like a violent storm, eerily reminiscent of the fit our Elizabeth suffered during the journey here. The woman's eyes, clouded with pain, focus on two girls beside her—one about seven, clutching a ragged doll, and the other just a toddler with chubby cheeks. Her hand reaches out, trembling, before it falls limp, and the life drains from her eyes.

The vision shifts, and now the two girls occupy separate beds, their small bodies frail and trembling with the same relentless symptoms. Their shallow breaths fade, and their eyes close, leaving a haunting emptiness that jolts me back to the present. My heart pounds in my chest as the reality of their loss hits me.

"Another vision?" Elizabeth's voice breaks through the haze, her eyes searching mine.

I nod, unable to speak, my throat tight with emotion.

"Are you okay, Claudia?" Mary's voice is gentle but edged with concern. "You look as if you've seen a ghost."

"I guess I kind of did—well, three actually," I reply, my voice barely above a whisper.

Mary gasps, her eyes widening in shock.

"All the more reason for us to begin the counterspell against the curse," Elizabeth insists, urgency sharpening her words.

Elizabeth's nostrils flare slightly with the mention of 'counterspell,' a subtle tension flickering across her face. Could it be mere coincidence that while Alex and I have been fending off Cromwell's counters, she now speaks of performing a 'counter' spell?

"Repeat after me," Elizabeth instructs, her tone firm and commanding. "I bind this curse with the unbreakable bonds of the Fates in the underworld and powerful Necessity."

As Mary clasps the stone she'd been handed, its surface gleaming with a faint sheen, she suddenly yelps and drops it to the ground. Elizabeth turns to her with a withering glare. "It became too hot to hold," Mary explains, her voice apologetic as she rubs her reddened fingers.

"Use your skirt to protect your hands," Elizabeth instructs, her voice steady and authoritative. "It must be held as you recite the words." Mary carefully wraps her hands in the fabric of her skirt, its delicate cotton brushing against her skin as she takes the stone again.

We gather around her, our voices merging into a single chant. Something feels amiss, a heaviness in the air. The Anna I knew, Elizabeth's reincarnated soul, used to be full of banter and lightheartedness, a spark in her eyes. But the woman before me now is somber, her eyes clouded with an unfamiliar seriousness.

"I invoke the innocent souls who passed too young. Rise yourselves and banish this curse," Elizabeth intones, her voice unwavering. We echo her words, our voices synchronized as though the spell has taken hold, transforming us into automatons. A shiver runs down my spine, a chill that prickles my skin.

"For with your help, I will bind this curse to these objects that we will bury near this sacred place," we repeat, following her outside into the crisp morning air. Barnabus, sturdy and reliable, digs a hole with a shovel Elizabeth brought along. He calls it a loy, and indeed it resembles a spade, its metal glinting in the light.

We place the cursed objects into the hollow earth, each piece a symbol of the darkness we seek to bury. Barnabus methodically covers the hole with dirt, the thud of each shovelful echoing in the quiet. Suddenly, a strong breeze sweeps through, lifting my hair and sending a shiver through me. We exchange glances, a silent understanding passing between us—I just know the curse has been lifted.

Our journey back is more relaxed, the tension that once gripped us now eased. The horses move comfortably beneath us, their saddles familiar and reassuring. Yet, a strange feeling lingers, a whisper of foreboding suggesting that, despite breaking the curse, something worse may still lie ahead.

As soon as we return, Fidelma and Líadan prepare to leave. Their farewells are hurried, urgency etched on their faces. "Grandma won't leave, but we have to try for her sake," Líadan says, her voice tinged with worry. "I don't want her here in case the battle does happen."

"There won't be a battle now that the curse is lifted," Elizabeth asserts, her words firm and confident.

"You don't know that," Mary counters, concern creasing her brow. "He still has ambitions, curse or no curse."

"I'll bet your grandma is up on the roof with her muskets waiting for them," Fidelma says to Líadan, a hint of amusement in her voice. "May Morrigan save their souls if they approach your house." Her words hang in the air, a mix of humor and grim reality.

Part of me longs to accompany them and meet Líadan's grandma, but I have a pressing task—I need to visit the tincture shop. Elizabeth's cough seems to be worsening each day, and we're here to ensure her safety and well-being. "I'm heading into town to do some shopping," I announce, glancing over at Elizabeth.

"Ride part of the way with me," Elizabeth suggests, her voice carrying a hint of urgency. "Help me with the horses."

"Are you going to be able to sneak them back in broad daylight?" I ask, my voice tinged with concern as I picture the watchful eyes of the camp.

Elizabeth gives me a reassuring smile. "Have a little faith. I have connections among my husband's men," she says with a confident nod.

Her assurance eases my worry, but a new concern arises. Does she expect me to handle two other horses while riding one?

"Don't worry," Elizabeth says, seemingly reading the apprehension in my furrowed brow. "They're well-trained horses."

As we approach the horses, Mary hurries over to intercept us. "Here," she says, pressing a necklace into each of our hands. "The pendants are delicate sculptures of leaves—birch, elder, and yew—crafted for protection."

Yep, that's my mother's soul all right, I think, feeling the familiar warmth of her intentions.

"You'll ride the same horse as before," Elizabeth instructs as Mary hurries back to join Barnabus at the house.

Once I'm mounted, Elizabeth brings over two more horses, their coats gleaming in the sunlight. "This pair is the friendliest," she assures me, handing me a rope that's secured to one horse and threaded through a loop on the other.

"It's only tied to one in case they break free," Elizabeth explains, noticing my scrutiny of the rope. "This way, there's less chance of them colliding together."

Every muscle in my body is as tight as a coiled spring as I follow Elizabeth's instructions, gripping the reins with white-knuckled fingers. "Relax," she advises, her voice calm and steady, as if it's as simple as flipping a switch. "It will go better for you if you're calmly in control." I take a deep breath, trying to mimic her poised demeanor, and for a while, it works. The horses move in unison, their hooves beating a rhythmic pattern against the dirt path. But then, they become distracted, their ears flicking toward distant sounds. Elizabeth guides her horses closer to mine and slows until she's beside me, unfortunately on my deaf side.

Her words become muddled, lost to the wind, so I focus on the horses instead, reading their subtle movements, the twitch of an ear, the swish of a tail, and try to lead them with instinct rather than sound. "This is where we part," Elizabeth announces as we near the ancient drawbridge, her voice clear now that she's positioned back on my hearing side, much to my relief. She takes my rope as I awkwardly swing my leg over and dismount, feeling the earth solid beneath my boots. A man in worn leather approaches, his presence unexpected, and I gasp.

"Fear not, Miss," he assures me, his voice as warm as the sun filtering through the trees. "I'm not a fighter, only here to protect the horses the best I can. They're innocent in all of this."

"Well, you're right about that," I reply, handing him my horse's reins. With practiced ease, he mounts as if it's second nature. Watching Elizabeth and the man ride off, I feel a weight lift from my shoulders, relieved not to see any ominous aura trailing behind him.

My gaze drifts to the bustling docks before landing on the row of quaint shops. Perhaps I can stop and visit Alex and then head to the tincture shop. It would be a comforting pause after all the turmoil, to be with someone familiar and from my home timeline. Sunlight dances on the smooth water that I know will churn with chaos tomorrow if the battle proceeds. Hearing the lively, everyday sounds of the dock through my good ear is a bittersweet reminder of normalcy.

Alex spots me, and his bemused expression softens. His hand brushes softly against my cheek, a touch I hadn't realized I longed for until now. My heart races, each beat echoing in my chest, blood coursing vigorously through my veins. I inhale deeply, savoring the comforting scent of him. "I can't believe you're here," Alex says, his voice tinged with wonder. "What are you doing?"

"Heading to the tincture shop," I reply, my voice laced with concern. "Elizabeth has a bad cough."

"Oh, no. It's repeating, isn't it?" he says, his voice tinged with disbelief.

"We broke the curse!" I reassure him, determination in my voice.

"Conor tells me your mom and her friends bound Cromwell from doing harm," he says.

"Well, that's something. Did they bind the counters too?" I ask, a hint of worry creeping in.

"I don't know," Alex murmurs, pressing his lips gently against my hair, offering comfort.

"Are you coming back to work anytime soon?" Conor's voice cuts through the moment, sharp and impatient.

"Just give me a minute," Alex calls back, his voice firm but understanding. He slowly unwraps his arms from around me, his gaze lingering, eyes smoldering with warmth. My head spins slightly as he leans in, capturing my lips in a lingering kiss. Neither of us want to let go of this moment.

I wrap my arms tightly around his neck, holding him close, trying to anchor him in place. I feel his lips curve upward into a smile against mine. "I have to get back," he whispers reluctantly.

"Fine, I'll go shopping. Meet later?" I propose, my voice light yet hopeful.

"Don't lose yourself in a book again," he teases, a playful glint in his eyes.

"Never!" I reply with a laugh, playfully slapping his arm and stealing one last quick kiss before pulling away.

Marie/Laura, my mother, spoke of the tincture shop with admiration, calling it impressive. But as I step inside, I realize that word felt too small to describe what I'm seeing. Bottles with golden caps twinkle in the shafts of natural light streaming through the windows. Artful pottery adorn some of the shelves, alongside a section of small, square drawers with ornate knobs and neatly written labels.

A sliding ladder beckons, offering access to the highest shelves. My eyes catch on a section filled with green glass jars, sparking my curiosity. I hope they might contain a crude form of Penicillium, not exactly what I need yet, but perhaps mold collected from decaying vegetation or even from the very cave where we sleep.

Back in the 17th century, it was mostly used for poultices, and I know I'll have to purify it. Thankfully, this town has mastered the extraction of its vital components. History, I muse, often overlooks the contributions of the true founders.

I make my way to a shelf brimming with glistening stones and vibrant crystals. My fingers graze over a chunk of charcoal, its surface gritty and dark, as my eyes scan the shelves for any sign of imported Northern Bauxite. When my gaze falls upon a red, spongy-looking rock with a coarse texture, I know immediately it's what I seek, even though the label reads 'méine' or 'ore.'

I had expected the mercantile to stock the funnel, material, and bellows I need, but they were absent. Instead, I had spotted them earlier at the corner shop filled with books and curiosities, so I decide to head there.

While gathering my supplies at the corner shop, a leather-bound journal catches my eye. Its cover is embossed with intricate patterns, and I can't resist the allure. I snatch it up and settle into a nearby chair. As I set my belongings down, I open the journal, captivated by the pages within. Each page is filled with detailed drawings, illustrating depictions of magic and culture that are rich beyond imagination.

A loud clatter pulls me from the journal's spell. A man with broad shoulders and a barrel-like torso charges toward me, an intense aura streaming behind him. My heart races, pounding in my chest, but my mind remains sharp and focused.

I calculate the timing, waiting for the perfect moment to throw the chair into his path. One heartbeat, two, and on the third, I yank the chair. It clatters to the side instead of blocking his way. Damn! He's upon me, but I quickly grab his shoulders and somersault backward, using his momentum to flip him over and land on top of him.

Just as I prepare to shout or strike, Alex rushes over, his eyes wide with urgency. "I saw him. He's the third one, and when I noticed him heading your way, I followed."

"Get off me," the man grumbles, struggling beneath me.

"Fine, but you're not going anywhere," Alex asserts, placing his hands firmly on the man's shoulders, taking my place as I stand and collect myself.

"I was only coming to warn you," the man says, his voice earnest. "Two men from the enemy are searching for you. They could arrive any second."

"What do you mean?" I ask, shock tingling through my veins.

"How can we trust you?" Alex demands, his eyes narrowing suspiciously.

Suddenly, loud voices echo from outside. I follow the men's gaze to see two figures with intense aura streams pacing outside the window.

"That's them. We need to hide," the man urges, his voice laced with urgency.

"All right," I agree, hastily gathering my things, my heart still racing.

"I'd rather deal with one than two," Alex mutters, his voice barely audible over the creaking floorboards beneath our feet as we trail behind the man leading us toward the back of the shop. His gait is quick, purposeful.

As we approach a narrow door, the man calls out, "Judy, let us in the back room." Judy, a woman with silver-streaked hair and kind eyes, nods as if they share an unspoken understanding. She swings the door open, allowing us inside.

Once we're in the dimly lit room, the man presses a finger to his lips, signaling us to remain silent. His eyes dart around nervously, as if expecting something ominous to appear at any moment. His face, though lined with years, softens, and beneath the tension, there's a fleeting hint of a boyish grin, as though a laugh is just waiting to escape.

Suddenly, men's voices echo through the shop, their boots thundering against the wooden floor as they approach. Their tones are harsh, almost threatening, as they confront Judy. "Have you seen a young lass?" one demands, his voice carrying a gruff edge. "Tall with long, brunette hair."

Judy's response is calm, almost teasing. "Well, that could describe more than a dozen women in town," she says.

"Yeah, but have any of them been here today?" insists the other man, his voice even rougher.

"No, not today. Sorry, lads, would you like a book for your troubles?" she offers with a hint of sarcasm.

"Who has time to read? Enough of this place. We'll check on the dock," one grumbles as their footsteps begin to fade, the sound growing fainter and fainter until silence envelops us once more. The relief is palpable, though we remain still, waiting a moment longer before breaking the quiet.

"Why are you protecting me?" I ask, turning to the man beside us. "Who am I to you?"

He hesitates, glancing at the door before speaking. "I care for someone who cares about you," he replies, cautiously cracking the door open to peek outside.

"Yeah, and who's that?" Alex presses, his eyes narrowing as the man nods slightly and opens the door wider.

"I'd rather not break their confidence," he says, his voice low.

"That's okay," I interject, curiosity piquing. "How are you from the enemy camp but friends with the shop owner?"

"She's a wonderful woman who deserves to own this shop," he explains, admiration in his voice. "But if the English are successful..."

"So you won't fight with them?" Alex asks, a hint of anxiety creeping into his voice at the thought of violence, of the looming specter of war.

"No, I'll have to; otherwise, it would break my cover as an Irish spy," the man admits, determination etched in his features. "But there's a way we can prevent bloodshed."

"How?" I ask, leaning forward, eager to catch every word of his plan.

"Yeah, how?" Alex echoes, his curiosity mirroring my own.

"Take out the cannons so they can't get to the people," the man reveals, a glint of resolve in his eyes, as if the weight of this mission is one he bears willingly.

"How?" I ask repeatedly, my mind spinning in disbelief at the words he just uttered.

"If you can access the ship, you can remove the detonation capabilities," he explains, his eyes narrowing with urgency.

"That might be a bit difficult," Alex interjects, glancing toward the bustling harbor outside. "The ship's guarded round the clock from what we can see at the dock."

"Do we have a cannon of our own?" I ask, desperation creeping into my voice.

"That might work," the man nods, considering the possibility.

"If we can get one into position," Alex muses, his eyes darting around as if mapping out a plan. "We could use the stacks of cargo at the dock as cover."

"Great, you have a plan," the man says, his voice a mix of encouragement and haste. "I best be on my way."

"Wait," I blurt out as he turns to leave. "We didn't even get your name."

"A spy can't tell us his name," Alex says with a knowing smirk.

"Name's Lochlainn," the man replies, offering a firm handshake before slipping out the door.

As we step away from the dimly lit back room, our heads still swirling with the unexpected encounter, we're met by a panting Conor, his cheeks flushed from running.

"You left in a flash," he says, addressing Alex with a breathless grin. "Oh hi, Claudia."

"Yeah, I followed the spy," Alex explains, a hint of excitement in his eyes. "Turns out he's on our side."

"Oh, yeah?" Conor's eyebrows shoot up in interest.

"He suggested we bring a cannon of our own to take out theirs," Alex continues, nodding toward the docks.

"Well, you've found Alex," I say, gesturing to Conor. "Perhaps you can help find a cannon."

"Oh, that reminds me," Conor says suddenly, his face turning serious. "My mom stopped me as I was running off to catch you."

"And?" Alex prompts, sensing the tension in Conor's voice.

"Her new friend..." Conor hesitates, searching his memory. "Laura, yeah, she's missing."

"What?" I gasp, my heart skipping a beat.

"She should have met up with my mother and friends, but she didn't show," Conor explains, worry etched across his face.

I'm struck silent, my mind reeling. The edges of my vision blur as panic floods my senses. Where's my mother?

Guarded Time

CHAPTER FOURTEEN – ALEXANDER

"When mortal eye – our work shall spy,

And mortal ear – our dirge shall hear."

(*Flory Cantillon's Funeral* by T. Crofton Croker

Fairy & Folk Tales of Ireland by W.B. Yeats)

I slipped Claudia's arm around my shoulders, feeling her weight press into me as I steadied her trembling form. Conor shot me a questioning glance, eyebrows furrowed in confusion, unable to grasp why Laura's sudden disappearance had such a profound effect on Claudia. The truth—that Laura was Claudia's mother—was a secret shared only between us.

A thought nagged at me to reach out to Elizabeth or Mary for help with a locator spell, but I hesitated. They'd insist on seeing Laura once we found her, and that could lead to complications we couldn't afford. Besides, given Claudia's current fragile state, I doubted she could manage the spell on her own.

"Is your mom still at the dock?" I asked Conor, hoping for a lead.

"She might be. Let's go check," he replied, nodding toward the direction of the waterfront.

As we moved through the cobblestone streets lined with quaint buildings, my mind raced. Cromwell seemed a likely suspect to have taken Laura, but he was preoccupied with siege preparations. We had just seen all three known counters without Laura among them. Was there another counter we hadn't accounted for? If they always came in pairs, that would complicate things further.

Stories of this land flickered in my memory—tales of shadows lurking in the woods and the foreboding presence that clung to the air. Could Marie, or rather Laura, have been abducted by the fae? I recalled a tale Claudia had once shared about the fae's ability to shapeshift. Could one have appeared to Laura as a needy human, deceiving her into captivity? Or perhaps they were sheltering her, and our fears were misplaced.

"Conor," Étaín called out, her voice urgent as we approached. "We may have found someone who saw Laura."

Étaín gestured to the woman beside her, whose wide eyes darted nervously from side to side, her fear palpable.

"Maybe we can go somewhere more quiet?" Claudia suggested softly, taking the woman's hand in a comforting grip.

"There's an office just over there." I pointed, guiding them to a small, dimly lit room.

Once inside, the woman sank into a chair, her breaths steadying. "They took her," she whispered, her voice trembling. "The Sasanachs!"

"Where did they take her?" Claudia demanded, her voice edged with desperation, prompting an awkward glance from Étaín.

I gently placed my hand on Claudia's arm, easing her back ever so slightly, trying to calm the mounting tension.

The woman's eyes darted to Étaín, whose jaw tightened beneath an otherwise placid face. "On the drawbridge, to the camp," she whispered, fingers trembling against her skirt. "The man who took her... his eyes followed me and my boy like a wolf tracking lambs."

Claudia's voice cracked. "And you waited until NOW to tell someone?"

"I tried! No one understood who I was talking about until Róis found me." The woman's shoulders hunched inward.

I squeezed Claudia's elbow and guided her away. Her breath came in short bursts against my neck as I held her.

"We'll find her," I murmured into her hair.

"How?" Her voice was small, her fingers digging into my forearms.

Claudia's eyes, normally sharp and clear, had gone glassy. A muscle jumped in her jaw. I swallowed hard against the tightness in my throat.

"The spy might help us locate—"

"Elizabeth knows people in camp." She pulled away, already turning.

I caught her wrist. "Elizabeth can't see Laura."

"Haigh!" Conor slid beside us, eyes bright. "What if we take out the cannon first? Create chaos, then snatch Laura?"

Claudia's spine straightened. "Yes."

The word hung between us. I blinked at the sudden steel in her voice.

We hurried toward the docks, where a crowd had gathered. Liam walked slowly toward us, favoring his injured side.

"Conor, Alex, look!"

My foot caught on nothing. Beside me, Conor's breath hitched audibly. Only Claudia remained still, her face a perfect mask. There, stood Hugh—flesh and blood—when just the other day we'd watched him fall.

"Heileo, Alex, Conor!" Hugh's voice boomed over the clatter of crates and the murmur of onlookers on the wharf. He grabbed my shoulder with a grip that rattled my ribs, then spun to Conor.

Conor's jaw dropped so hard I could almost hear the crack. He jabbed a finger into Hugh's chest—hard enough to leave a bruise. "You're—you're alive?" His disbelief tasted of bitter ale on the breeze.

Hugh shrugged, the light dancing across his soot-streaked face. "I don't know how, but I'm fine." He brushed ash from his coat sleeve.

Conor's brow furrowed. "Wait—haven't you handled a cannon before?"

From behind us, Rí folded his arms, boots thudding on the planks. "Why in God's name do you ask about a cannon?" His gaze flicked to Hugh, then to me.

We slipped away from the milling crowd and ducked into Teach Chairbre, the tavern's speciality for the day creaking in the wind. Inside, the air was thick with wood smoke and the tang of spilled ale. Leann appeared from the shadows carrying a skillet piled high with steaming fadge—round, golden potato bread that hissed softly as she set it before us. Before Liam could open his mouth for ale, she'd already sloshed mugs to the bar with a grin.

I tore off a chunk of the warm bread, fingers dusted with flour, and asked Hugh, voice low above the crackle of the hearth, "So—how would we stop a cannon?"

Hugh propped his elbows on the scarred table. "First, you must reach it."

Liam leaned forward, eyes bright. "Don't worry—Conor and I will handle getting aboard that ship." He wiped fadge crumbs from his barely visible beard.

Claudia folded back the linen napkin. "But once we're there?"

Hugh lifted a twisted iron spike from a pouch at his belt. The barbs glint like broken teeth. "Drive this into the touchhole. Barbs keep it lodged. No powder, no boom."

We traced routes on a scrap of parchment by lantern light, despite Claudia's urgent whispers that we rescue Laura now. Liam thumped the table. "I'll distract the gun crews—send their food tumbling into the river. The current'll carry it downstream, and they'll chase it like dogs."

"Then Rí and Conor slip aboard, spike the touchhole, and we vanish before anyone notices," I added, voice tight. "By the time they chip out those barbs, hours will have slipped past— hours for Claudia and me to sneak into the camp."

Claudia nodded, jaw set. But all of us felt the weight of exhaustion dragging at our shoulders. Liam rubbed his temples. "Let's rest. Some of us are still smelling of tavern floor."

There was availability, so Claudia and I shared a room at the inn down the street. The door creaked behind us as we entered a small chamber warmed by a glowing hearth. A canopy bed draped in faded tapestries dominated the room; its wrought-iron chains sagged softly against the posts.

I sunk onto a padded wooden chair, unlacing my boots until my feet hit the rough-hewn floor. Claudia kicked off her own boots and bounded onto the mattress, tossing a pillow over her shoulder.

She turned, eyes bright, and wrapped a hand around the nape of my neck before I could think. Warmth and urgency collided as her lips found mine.

"Claudia," I murmured against her mouth, heart hammering, "we need rest."

She pulled back only a breath. "How can I sleep while my mother rots in their cages?"

I cupped her cheek, voice soft. "Because tomorrow we free her. But only if we're sharp."

Her lips curved. "Then let me forget everything else…" She trailed kisses down my jaw and across my throat until reason dissolved.

I wrapped my arms around her, pulling her tightly against me, feeling the warmth of her body align with mine. As she deftly untied the laces of my tunic, her silky hair brushed lightly against my collarbone, sending a shiver down my spine. When Claudia leaned in and parted my lips with her own, an overwhelming realization surged through me, knocking the breath from my lungs—this intimate connection was something we both desperately needed.

Her heart fluttered against my chest like the rapid wings of a butterfly, its rhythm echoing my own. My fingers roamed her skin, exploring each curve and dip as she undressed. Her skin was like velvet beneath my touch, irresistible in its allure. I traced the gentle slope of her shoulder, down to the tender skin beneath her arm and the soft curve under her breast. Her sudden, sharp intake of breath was a tantalizing sound that heightened the moment.

Our next kiss was searing, sparking a fire deep within me that blazed with intensity. My hands followed the line of her spine, finally resting at the small of her back, feeling the delicate arch beneath my palms. She pressed her lips to my neck, trailing kisses behind my ear, and whispered my name, a sound that made my heart race. I kissed her with a hunger that couldn't be sated, as she tilted her head back, surrendering to the passion between us. Being with her was all-consuming, a liberation in the privacy of our room, free to explore and discover each other without restraint.

After what felt like the most blissful night of my life, we drifted into sleep, entwined and bare, with the comfort of a soft bed beneath us instead of the hard rock floor. As we finally stirred, the scent of Claudia lingered in the air, a heady fragrance that I wished to linger in forever. Yet, the gentle drift of sunlight through the canopy above reminded me of the world outside, urging us to rise.

I bolted upright. "We overslept."

Claudia's eyes flew open. She leapt from the bed, yanking her dress over her head, cursing under her breath. Her fingers raked through her tangled hair, leaving it wilder than before.

"What?" She caught me watching her. "We're going to miss our chance. Move!"

The dock swarmed with bodies, a sea of coats and metal buttons glinting in the morning light. Rí's face was grim as he pushed through the crowd toward us, Conor and Liam at his heels.

"Aston refused," Liam panted, his knuckles white around his bow.

Claudia shoved past them toward the water. The air cracked open. Stone and mortar rained down where the steeple had stood unmarred moments before. I pulled her against me as another blast shook the ground beneath our feet. The crowd froze, faces pale, eyes wide.

Boom after boom. The steeple crumbled more and more. Dust clouded the air.

"The wall?" Liam's voice cracked.

Rí shook his head. "They'll rest tonight. That wall has stood for a hundred years."

"Then we strike at nightfall," Conor whispered, eyes gleaming.

Claudia's chest heaved as we gathered at the dock. Moonlight slashed through ragged clouds, turning the wooden planks silver and black. Liam's voice cut the stillness. "We're going by boat across the water."

Rí ducked under a lantern's glow, fingers tracing the grain of the railing. "We'll go without light, so they don't spot us. Conor and I know the currents by heart."

Conor smacked an oar handle between his gloved hands. "And we'll row as quietly as we can."

He helped Claudia and me into a skiff while Liam and Rí settled into another. The oars slipped into the water with soft, urgent taps that set my teeth on edge. Mist drifted over the river like pale smoke, hiding our progress but stealing every landmark.

Claudia's fingers curled around mine, cool and shaking. I squeezed back, sharing her fear and drawing strength from it. Stars winked overhead, powerless against the fog.

After what felt like hours, our hulls scraped a muddy bank. Conor crouched low at the stern, jaw clenched. He was ready for a new action—but the old plan of tossing food over the rail wouldn't work under cover of night.

Claudia leaned close. "Are you worried you won't knock the men aboard out?"

Conor swallowed so hard I saw his Adam's apple jump. "No," he whispered, voice rough. "I'm afraid I'll do more than knock them out."

Liam snorted softly. "It's war. They asked for this when they attacked our home."

Conor's gloved fingers trembled around the sword at his belt. Claudia laid her palm over his, warm and steady. Luckily, the glove kept her from being overwhelmed with the sight. She rose to her full height, moonlight outlining her in silver.

"I call upon the Goddess Macha," she intoned.

Rí's brow shot up. "Not the Ulster curse!"

Claudia silenced him with a fingertip to her lips. "It's altered. Let Cromwell's men be overcome with sleep so they shall not rise for nine hours."

Liam folded his arms. "Nine hours?"

Conor's lips curved into a slow grin. He vaulted onto the nearest ship and slapped the first sentry he found. The man slumped against the rail, unmoving. We all held our breath until at last—nothing. The soldier sat still in the moonlight.

Relief washed over us. Liam's grin gleamed. "Perfect. Now, with time on our side, let's block every cannon! Why didn't you do this earlier—or make the spell longer?"

Claudia's eyes flashed. "They're hunting witches. If I'd woven a stronger enchantment, every woman in town would be under suspicion."

Rí bowed his head. "Understood. Thank you, Claudia." Then he turned to Liam. "Where's the blacksmith's tent?"

I hesitated as Conor climbed back down. "Do you need me to stay?"

Conor scoffed. "Leave Claudia to rescue Laura alone, surrounded by soldiers?"

Claudia brushed a stray hair from her face. "Did you see how deep they sleep?" She smiled. "We've got this."

"I'm sure you would manage just fine," Rí assured Claudia with a gentle nod. "But because of you, Conor can lend a hand now, and I'm not keen on anyone being left alone." Claudia's frown softened, and she seemed more at ease.

As she and I navigated through the bustling camp, I took in the scene: rows of tents flanked by makeshift shelters constructed from branches and tarps leaned against tree trunks. Upside-down crates served as tables, scattered with playing cards and dice, while the air was thick with the smell of damp earth. The place had a worn, rough-around-the-edges feel. Who would volunteer for such a life?

"They all look the same," Claudia murmured, her voice tinged with frustration. "How are we going to find her?"

"There are a few larger tents," I pointed out, scanning the area. "One of them might belong to the quartermaster, storing essential supplies. We could disrupt their operations while we search."

She chuckled, a mischievous glint in her eye. "Tempting, but let's split up. Maybe one of those bigger tents is Cromwell's. I bet my mother is held close by."

"Let's stick together, just in case," I suggested, glancing around cautiously.

"Fine!" she agreed with a reluctant sigh.

We ducked into the first large tent, and my guess was right—shelves and piles of supplies lined the canvas walls. Spotting a row of boots, I darted over and began threading twine through the buckles, my knife flashing as I cut lengths of string.

"What are you doing?" Claudia asked, eyebrow raised.

"I'm going to toss them onto the highest branches outside," I explained, tying buckles together with precision.

"Why don't you cut, and I tie? It'll go faster," she proposed.

I handed her strips of twine and grinned. "Just make sure to leave enough slack so they'll catch around the branches."

With a dozen pairs tied tightly, we stepped outside and flung them skyward, the boots swinging and catching on branches. Claudia's laughter rang out, light and contagious.

"Okay, let's head to the next tent," Claudia suggested, eyes bright with excitement.

"Just need to dump their coffee first," I replied, glancing back toward the tent.

We dashed back and forth, hauling cannisters to the door and emptying their contents onto the ground, the rich aroma of coffee mingling with the earth.

"Too bad I can't summon rain," Claudia mused, smirking. "There isn't enough time to create steam."

"Wait, you can actually do that?" I asked, surprised.

She shrugged, a mysterious smile playing on her lips. Her magic had deepened here, as though she was truly connected to this land. It made sense, considering it was where her soul originated.

We made our way to the next large tent, its canvas walls barely containing the stockpile of arms and ammunition inside. The rancid scent of gun tallow mixed with the sharp tang of gunpowder filled the air. I approached a barrel along the wall, pried open its lid, and found it brimming with gunpowder. The dark grains glistened ominously under the dim light. Grabbing a nearby pail, I plunged it into the barrel, scooping up the explosive powder. Claudia, standing beside me, picked up another pail.

"Tossing it on the coffee?" she asked, her eyebrows raised in a conspiratorial arch.

"Exactly!" I replied, flashing a grin as we both filled our pails with the black powder.

After scattering the gunpowder, I remarked, "It's going to be more difficult for some of them to wake from their slumber now."

"Can we please try to find Cromwell's tent?" Claudia pleaded, her voice tinged with urgency.

"Yeah, let's just toss the buckets back in the weapons tent," I said, pointing to the doorway.

"Why?" she questioned, confusion flickering across her face.

Before I could explain, a sharp voice pierced the air. A woman in a nurse's uniform came charging at us, her eyes blazing with determination. "Oh, no you don't," she shouted, her voice a mix of authority and anger. "There won't be any thieving on my watch."

Suddenly, a jolt of pain shot through my side as something sharp pierced my flesh. Gasping, I crumpled to my knees, clutching my side. Claudia reacted swiftly, swinging her pail with all her might and striking the woman on the head. The nurse crumpled to the ground, and in a haze of adrenaline and fear, I toppled backward.

"Alex," Claudia's voice reached me, thick with concern. "Alex, are you okay?"

"Claudia!" Marie's voice cut through my disoriented state, drawing my gaze to where she was bound in chains. I had stumbled into the exact tent we needed. "What are you doing here? You shouldn't be here. They're looking for you."

"We're here to set you free, Mother," Claudia declared with fierce determination. "But Alex got stabbed."

Glancing down, I saw the gleaming blade protruding from my side, each throb reminding me of its presence. Desperate to stay conscious, I forced myself to speak. "How was she not asleep?" I croaked, each word a struggle.

"Because I idiotically only cursed Cromwell's men!" Claudia admitted, frustration coloring her voice.

"Claudia, you what?" Marie demanded, her voice a mix of disbelief and urgency.

"There's no time," Claudia insisted, worry tightening her features. "I must set you free so you can help me heal him."

With determination, Claudia moved to Marie's side, examining the chains that bound her. She assessed the stake anchoring the chains to the ground and gave it a decisive kick.

"Ow!"

"There's a mallet in the last tent we were in," I said, trying to keep my voice steady despite the pain.

She hurried over with a lantern flickering in her hand and a bundle of cloth under her arm. The warm glow cast soft shadows across her face as she knelt beside me. Gently lifting my tunic, she inspected the wound with a careful eye. "It's not bleeding too bad, and it didn't hit any major organs," she murmured, her fingers lightly tracing the area around the knife.

"How do you know that?" I asked, my curiosity piqued despite the situation.

Her eyes flickered with a distant, thoughtful look. "My memories from other timelines are becoming clearer. You and I worked at a lab in one of them."

"Really?" I replied, surprised.

"Yeah, you were my mentor then." She handed me the cloth, her fingers brushing mine as she guided my hand to the knife. "Don't press hard, just keep it there," she instructed, her tone gentle but firm.

The mere thought of applying pressure sent a wave of discomfort through me. I nodded, knowing I wouldn't have any trouble following her orders. She turned and dashed out of the tent, her silhouette quickly swallowed by the night.

"How could you let her talk you into this?" Marie's voice cut through the quiet, full of reproach.

"Do you really think I could have persuaded her against it?" I countered, a slight smile tugging at my lips.

"You're right, she's always been strong-willed…at least with me," Marie admitted, her voice softening.

"She loves you," I said sincerely.

"That's kind of you to say."

"It's the truth," I replied.

Claudia reappeared, her silhouette framed by the lantern light. She carried a mallet in one hand and what looked like a first-aid kit in the other. Setting the kit down beside me, she moved with purpose to where Marie stood. She raised the mallet and struck the stake from one side, the upward angle seeming awkward at first. I opened my mouth to suggest a different approach, but she had already adjusted, shifting to the other side with precision.

Marie's eyes darted between me and the stake. "Care for him first," she insisted, her voice tight. "This is going to take too long."

Claudia's fingers trembled slightly as she peeled away the blood-soaked fabric from my side. The air hit the wound, and I hissed through clenched teeth.

"Wine?" She gestured toward a dusty bottle in the corner.

I tried to follow her gaze, but the slight movement sent lightning through my ribs. I managed a jerky nod.

The liquid burned going down, spilling over my chin as she tipped the cup. Every swallow pulled at torn flesh.

She uncorked a cloudy bottle from the kit. The sharp vinegar scent made my nostrils flare.

"How do you—"

"Label." A tight smile flickered across her face. "Deep breath. Knife out, solution in, pressure after."

My fingernails dug half-moons into my palms as she gripped the handle. One quick motion and the room spun, ceiling and floor trading places. The solution hit next—acid in an open wound. When the cloth pressed down, pinpricks of darkness swarmed like insects at the edges of my vision.

"What's next?" My voice sounded distant, underwater.

She guided my hand to hold the cloth. "Stitches."

The needle glinted as she rinsed it. Once. Twice. Three times. Her knuckles white around the thread.

"I love you," I whispered as the sharp object approached my skin.

"Love you too." Her voice steady, her hands not. "Almost done."

The needle pierced, and darkness rushed in like tidewater. Each stitch pulled me further under until there was nothing but the fading echo of pain and then, mercifully, nothing at all.

CHAPTER FIFTEEN – MARIE

"Is he all right?" I ask Claudia, my voice cracking with worry as I glance at Alex's still form on the dirt floor.

"His heartbeat and breathing are steady," she says, pressing two fingers against his neck. "He'll be just fine."

She comes back over to me, her leather boots leaving deep imprints in the dirt, and picks up the heavy oak mallet. As she swings at the iron stake, I notice the sinewy muscles rippling beneath her sun-touched skin—muscles she's acquired during our time in Drogheda.

Once the stake comes free with a sucking sound from the wet earth, I'm finally able to release my arms, the skin raw where the chains had pressed. After I rub the soreness out of them, feeling pins and needles shoot through my fingertips, I give her one of the biggest hugs I've ever given her in her life, breathing in the scent of gunpowder and sweat in her tangled hair.

"It was no problem, Mom," she says, her voice muffled against my shoulder. "You would have done the same for me."

"Catch me up on what's going on," I say, pulling back to look at her dirt-streaked face. "I heard and felt the cannons from here—the ground shook like an earthquake."

"Cromwell's taken the steeple and put a hurting on the eastern wall. There's almost a breach near the old monastery."

I bend over with my hands on my knees, my stomach churning with nausea. "It's really happening, the siege all over again. I don't know if I can stomach it."

"Was it that horrible?" she asks, her eyes—so like her father's—wide with concern.

"Yes," I whisper, the memories flooding back like a crimson tide. "It was a slaughter! Bodies piled in the streets, the river running red..."

"Well, we may have put a dent in Cromwell's plans," she says, squaring her shoulders with newfound confidence.

She tells me about how they blocked cannon touchholes with iron spikes, threw out coffee grounds and mixed them with gunpowder to sabotage their weapons, and that Alex's crew would still be at it for a while longer, working under the cover of darkness.

In the short time we've been here, my daughter has grown more than I ever could have imagined. The young woman from Kansas City has been replaced by this warrior with calloused hands and fierce determination. I wonder how that will change the timelines, the delicate threads of fate we've been manipulating.

That reminds me of how Cromwell wants me to reincarnate only him and Elizabeth—his cold eyes gleaming with selfish ambition as he outlined his plan. If I don't reincarnate Barnabus and myself, the gift won't pass to Claudia's original soul, and the daughter standing before me now, with her father's chin and my stubbornness, will not exist.

"And what have you been doing while stuck here?" Claudia asks me, wiping a smudge of dirt from her cheek. "I hope he hasn't been too horrible to you."

"Oh, I can handle him," I say with a brittle laugh. "But I'm not sure I can handle what he's planning."

"Do tell!" she exclaims, leaning forward eagerly.

"He wants me to reincarnate only Elizabeth and himself—not Barnabus or myself," I explain, watching her face closely for reaction.

"That would mean it wouldn't pass to me..." she whispers, her face paling beneath its burn. "And I'd never meet Alex!"

She paces the tent, her boots wearing a path in the packed earth, checking on Alex too, her fingers gently brushing his forehead.

"Maybe I can try conjuring it on myself now!" I say suddenly.

Her eyes flash with determination as she raises her hands, fingers splayed as if already feeling the magic coursing through them. Standing next to me, she asks, "Would you like my help?"

"When I did this last time, I did it alone, so…" my words drift off as Claudia shoulders lift and fall in silent resignation.

I straighten, planting my feet firmly on the packed earth. "I call upon the Goddess Ariannhod," I declare, my voice low and steady, like a bell tolling in a quiet chapel. I draw in a trembling breath, heart hammering beneath my ribs. My fists clench before me, knuckles white. "I don't have much to offer you now," I admit, "but I have bestowed blessings throughout my timelines as tokens of my gratitude."

Behind me, the tent fabric ripples as if stirred by an unseen breeze—though no wind blows through this sheltered space. I recall the Welsh scholar who once passed through our town, his stories of Ariannhod spoken in lilting tones, the faint scent of peat clinging to his cloak. I kneel on the coarse blanket underfoot, the fibers prickling my skin.

"Ariannhod, Silver Wheel, we kneel—

Your children seeking truth beneath your gaze,

In this Earth-Circle open to the stars,

Rebirth understanding, heal our wounded days."

Candles waver around us, their flames flicking erratically before some sputter and die, though the air remains unnaturally still. A prickle of unease crawls up my spine. Claudia drops to her knees beside me, her warm presence a comfort in the dim glow.

"Veiled and unveiled, you contain

Earth's body, Moon's face—never apart.

You are magic bridging soil and sky,

The ancient power dwelling in your heart."

As my final words echo, the air shifts again—but this time it slumps inward, as though the tent itself is inhaling. The remaining candles gutter, yet stubbornly refuse to snuff out completely. A hollow ache blooms in my chest.

"Something's not right," I whisper, voice taut.

Claudia's brow furrows. "It felt strong to me," she says, offering a small, encouraging smile.

I force a calm breath, brushing stray hair from my face. Memories of other selves—other lifetimes—swirl just beyond reach, hazy as smoke. Even the recollection of Claudia in those timelines is thinning, slipping away like footprints in sand.

"Maybe I'm just stressed," I lie, forcing a rational tone.

"Here, give this to Elizabeth if you see her." Claudia hands me a vial. "I have one too. They contain medicine that she needs."

Then Claudia rises, urgency in her eyes. "I need to check on him—get him conscious and wrap him up so we can move." She unclips a small vial of smelling salts and holds it beneath his nose; the sharp ammonia burns the air. His eyelashes flutter, then his arms jerk as he tries to lift himself by his elbows.

"Easy," Claudia murmurs, guiding him gently.

He blinks rapidly, voice gravelly. "Where are we?"

"In Cromwell's tent," Claudia answers, concern lacing her tone. "You were stabbed by a nurse from his regiment."

"Oh, right." He winces, the memory returning in flashes of pain.

Claudia sinks to one knee, tilts his head upright, and holds a finger before his eyes. "Follow my finger," she instructs softly, moving it in a slow horizontal arc. His gaze follows without lag, pupils tracking smoothly. Satisfied, she helps him into a sitting position.

She pulls a roll of bandage from her medical kit—cool antiseptic smell rising as she wraps his torso with expert hands. While they work, I retreat into my thoughts, staring at the dim candlelight flickering against the canvas. If I can no longer call forth Ariannhod's grace, what becomes of me? Claudia's magic grows with every passing hour—surely mine should not be dwindling.

I've often read in fantasy novels about how a mother witch's magic diminishes as her daughter's grows, but I had never witnessed it in reality. Until now, perhaps. If that's what's happening, I'm genuinely happy for Claudia, but I wish we weren't mired in this chaotic mess.

The danger is palpable here. I don't need to glance at Alex's bandaged wound or the stake I was once chained to, to understand the peril we're in. The thought crosses my mind: could I send us back to the Prohibition Era in Kansas City? It might be our safest bet. We've hardly made progress here, after all.

However, to pull off such a feat, I'd require the cooperation of a few people. Would my coven believe me if I revealed the truth? And even if they did, would they agree to help us leave just when we seem so crucial to their cause? Is it right for me to even suggest it?

I doubt Claudia and Alex would want to leave now. They've achieved some success in thwarting Cromwell's siege plans. Maybe it's time I confront what I've been avoiding and seek out Mary. Or perhaps I could persuade Alex to convince Claudia to enlist Mary's help for a time travel spell… at least for their sake.

"How's he doing?" I ask Claudia, glancing at Alex's form.

"I'll be right as rain before you know it," Alex assures me with a faint smile, slipping back into his familiar vernacular— no one in the 17th century uses phrases like 'right as rain.'

A hare hops through the tent flap, despite Claudia having carefully moved Alex further inside. The creature's eyes catch the candlelight, creating an eerie reflection as if the flame were more than just a flame. It's a surreal moment. Then, an unfamiliar sensation washes over me as I feel my consciousness lift away from my body.

I hear Claudia calling my name, but her voice sounds distant and muffled, fading into silence. Am I being spirited away by a faery? The scene around me swirls, colors blending and transforming until I find myself seated in a pergola, clutching a framed photo. Austria, Claudia from another timeline, is there beside me, gently squeezing my shoulder.

The wooden slats above me blur into a whirl of sun-bleached brown and drifting ivy. When I pry my eyelids open, a glossy black piano stretches before me, its lid propped open like a raven's wing. I settle onto the leather bench, feet pressing into cool steel pedals, hands hovering over ivory keys. As soon as I let my fingers fall, a ribbon of melody unfurls—familiar scales weaving through me as though I'd practiced this piece yesterday, not across two fractured timelines. Still, each chord wraps around my chest like the softest blanket, comforting and strange.

A scent of white roses drifts in, and I'm back at Austria's wedding. The pews are lined with glittering pomanders—tiny globes of blooms suspended by satin ribbon, swaying with every hushed murmur. I see her in a gown and Josh, reincarnated Alex, in a hand-me-down tux, their hands entwined as they mount the steps. Between them hangs an embroidered banner, threads of gold and ivory twisting into delicate filigree. I wanted so badly to tell Claudia then what I know now—warn her of the shadows slipping through our lives—but I clamped my lips shut. I thought I was protecting her. In reality, I buried her in questions she had to answer alone. She unraveled truths at her own peril; the darkness trailing her like a predator.

In that world, Elizabeth stood at Claudia's side as grandmother, a role that never belonged to her in my original life. My vision wavers, smudges of light and dark bleeding together until everything fades.

Silence swells, a thick vacuum. Gone are the resonant chords, the click of the piano lid. My pulse hammers so loud I can't hear my own thoughts. My arms feel weightless until a gentle pressure grips my hand—an unseen presence guiding me forward.

The ground twists beneath my feet. One moment it's like I'm plummeting down a grassy hill, wind scorching my cheeks. The next, as if I'm thrown against the seat of a rattling truck, the road's bones trembling up my spine. But when I open my eyes, I'm strapped into a slim cockpit of steel and glass, stars flickering past like fireflies. My skin prickles as if every charged particle in the universe recoils from me. This leap carries me three lifetimes removed.

My muscles go slack, and I crumble onto a narrow gurney, white sheets crisp beneath me. I ache for our telepathy—how I could have reached Claudia across any void with a thought. In that lifetime, words weren't necessary. Now, my mind stalls, craving that silent line of connection.

Here, they engineered clones, non-bios, soul-spliced transplants. I carried twins once—my sons—until Cromwell claimed one for his dark experiments and the government seized the other. When Claudia's clone emerged, trembling and wide-eyed, I wrapped her in my arms and vowed she was mine, regardless of her origin. She needed that truth, even if I once withheld it.

My bones feel bruised from every skirmish we've fought across time's fractured veins. If the faery comes for me now, let her at least guide me back to a moment of pure light—one last happy memory before the shadows swallow me whole.

Now, a vivid flash from my memory surfaces—racing toward my daughters as danger loomed, our eyes locking in a moment of silent understanding, conveying a thousand unspoken words. The adrenaline of those moments, riding in sleek poli-magnos and soaring on hovers, binds us in an unbreakable bond. These memories remind me of the chain of events that led us here. Claudia, in another timeline, had ended Cromwell's life, sparking the creation of the counter world and the counters themselves. I wonder if I could reach her telepathically before she makes that fateful choice.

"Vienna, don't send the transformed images of Cromwell being tortured." Something about it feels wrong, like a dissonant chord in an otherwise harmonious melody. I doubt my plea reached her across the expanse of worlds.

Before I can fully process my thoughts, I'm caught in a whirlwind of sensations and emotions, unfamiliar powers slipping into my consciousness like tendrils of mist. This must be the counter world—a place filled with faces and energies I don't recognize.

Abruptly, my surroundings change. Instead of swirling, I'm drawn upward, pulled into a hidden chamber at the end of a dimly lit hallway. Shadows obscure my view until a faint glow reveals a room shrouded in mystery. There, resting on the dusty floor, is a journal with a cracked leather cover—my own.

Could the key to my inability to cast reincarnation or connect telepathically lie within these pages? Yet, there's no time to sift through them, and who knows which of my journals would hold the answer?

The distant strains of Samhain festival music drift to my ears, a scene I've glimpsed before from the counter time world. The air is thick with an ancient, potent energy, blending the past with the present in this modern age. The festival, meant to celebrate, turns eerily macabre, echoing a poor imitation of a siege from long ago.

People gather around a looming lighthouse, clad in elaborate costumes and glinting armor. The flickering candlelight casts a warm glow on their eager faces, but soon the ghostly howls rise, chilling the air. The sudden blaze of a towering bonfire renders the candles superfluous, casting long shadows that dance in the flickering light.

The vision of thick rope threaded through silver claddagh rings, binding aromatic bundles of lavender, brings the salty, bracing scent of the sea. As the lavender bundles are tossed into the crackling fire, the flames leap, and suddenly, I'm spinning in a dizzying whirl. The sensation fades, and I find myself back inside Cromwell's dim canvas tent.

Claudia leans over me, her eyes full of concern, holding a small vial of smelling salts under my nose. "Finally," she breathes, relief in her voice. "I couldn't wake you for a long time."

Alex stands nearby, his tall frame slightly hunched, his eyes scanning my face.

"I'm fine," I assure them, though my voice wavers. "Just had an out-of-body experience or something."

"It was much more than a second," Claudia retorts, a touch of exasperation in her voice.

Outside, muffled voices grow louder, disrupting the tent's stillness.

"They're waking," Claudia says, glancing toward the canvas entrance.

Without missing a beat, Alex grasps Claudia's hand, and they move instinctively toward the tent flap. Their connection is palpable, an unspoken bond that guides their synchronized movement. The flap swishes open, and they disappear into the fading light.

I attempt to follow, but my legs feel unsteady, still reeling from the faery's flight. My foot catches on a loose rope, and I crash to the ground. The voices outside the tent grow clearer, instantly recognizable, and not in a pleasant way. It's the counters. I scramble to my feet, heart racing, desperate to escape before they find me.

My hand reaches for the tent flap, but it opens before I can touch it. Standing there are two of the last faces I want to encounter in the world.

"What are you doing up and about?" Ruarc demands, his eyes narrowing suspiciously.

"It doesn't matter," Aodhán interjects. "I'm done with Cromwell's orders anyway."

"Trouble at home?" I ask, intrigued by the possibility of their discontent.

"Don't tell her anything," Ruarc snaps, casting a warning glance at Aodhán.

"Maybe she could help," Aodhán counters, his voice softer, tinged with hope.

"What are you talking about?" I press, curiosity piqued.

They begin to pace restlessly in the confined space of the tent, sharing their grievances against Cromwell. Their words tumble out in a torrent of frustration, painting a picture of a man consumed by his vision, a zealous leader intent on forging a stifling theocracy.

In their eyes, he carried his genocidal tendencies from this original timeline into all others. Initially, they saw him as a transformative figure, someone who could eliminate corruption across eras. But hypocrisy seemed to cling to him like a shadow—from champion of parliamentary freedoms to dismissing parliaments he disagreed with by force, and from advocating religious tolerance to slaughtering those of a faith he despised. How were they supposed to pacify a man with such a duplicitous nature?

"We beg of you to help set us free from a tyrant," Aodhán implores, his voice heavy with desperation.

"Are you in agreement?" I ask Ruarc, turning to him for confirmation.

He nods solemnly, but I feel overwhelmed by the enormity of the task—how can I possibly free them from the grip of Cromwell?

"How do you propose I do this?" I inquire, hoping they have a plan.

"When he asks you to reincarnate him," Ruarc suggests, his eyes lighting up with a cunning plan, "slip a different spell in with it."

I recall the bay leaves Cromwell had burned to nullify the binding spell my coven had cast. "Perhaps there's something we can do now," I suggest, feeling a glimmer of hope.

They both lean forward eagerly, hanging onto my every word. "Spit it out already," Aodhán urges impatiently.

"He's been burning bay leaves," I explain. "Do you know where he keeps them?"

Sitting at the table, I notice the quill and ink Cromwell had used not long ago. Once Ruarc returns with a handful of leaves, I inscribe an affirmation on one, declaring that he will set the two men free, and then I burn the leaf, watching the smoke curl upward.

Next, I prepare to write an affirmation about how he'll cease harming others and leave those I care for unharmed, but just as I'm about to begin, the tent flaps open, and in strides Lochlainn. "Why is she out of chains?" he demands, eyeing the other two with suspicion.

He seizes my arm, dragging me back toward the stake. As he secures the chains around me, I notice his deliberate error, leaving them loose enough for me to escape in a heartbeat. Before turning away, he gives me a conspiratorial wink.

"You always ruin any fun we have," Ruarc grumbles at Lochlainn, frustration in his voice.

"Yeah, who gave you authority anyway?" Aodhán chimes in, echoing the sentiment.

Cromwell's shadow falls across the entrance first, followed by Elizabeth's slender silhouette beside him. A hare darts between their legs, its ears twitching nervously. Light flashes— blinding, disorienting—and my fingers grip the edge of my chair until my knuckles whiten.

The tent walls blur. Piano notes trickle through my consciousness like raindrops on glass. I see my sister's hands— flour-dusted, gentle—passing cookies to children whose eyes had once been hollow with fear. The same hands that had removed shackles in the world with poli-magnos, replacing torture manuals with textbooks, whispering encouragement where screams once echoed.

My stomach lurches as I remember her body, crumpled and still, my daughter's tear-streaked face above her. The memory spins away, leaving questions that taste like copper in my mouth.

I blink back to the present. Elizabeth's eyes meet Lochlainn's in silent communication before finding mine. Her chin lifts slightly—that familiar gesture of determination I've seen across centuries. Beside her, Cromwell's hand clenches and unclenches, unaware of how often her whispered midnight counsel has stayed his bloody impulses.

CHAPTER SIXTEEN – CROMWELL

"You have been sat too long here for any good you have been doing. Depart, I say, and let us have done with you. In the name of God, go!"

Cromwell addressing the rump Parliament. April 1653.

The day before Oliver's plan had been thrown off course, the water had surged with aggressive turbulence, yet the formation stood poised and defiant, ready to strike. The cannon barrel gleamed with a ruthless shine, meticulously cleaned so no speck of dirt or debris dared linger.

Across the expanse, Oliver's gaze locked onto Arthur and his troops, perched confidently on a hill behind the wall, their faces betraying a smug assurance. The thought of shattering their confidence into dust filled him with a fierce determination.

"Measure the gunpowder!" Oliver barked, his voice cutting through the noise like a blade.

Soldiers around him sprang into action, driven by the urgency of the command. The colossal transport ship glistened under the sun's harsh glare, packed from bow to stern with the lethal armory needed to obliterate the wall. Echoes of men shouting fervent encouragement to each other filled the air, a cacophony of impending doom.

A thunderous boom erupted as the first cannon shot exploded forth, a deep, earth-shattering detonation. Waves rippled violently across the water, their power undeniable. The shot screamed past the wall, slamming into the church with a catastrophic crash. Masonry rained down in a deadly shower after smashing into the towering steeple.

Oliver hoped this caused a rush of fear and confusion in his enemy. He needed to prevent musketeers from being able to shoot at his men once they finally made it past the godforsaken wall.

Thick tendrils of mist rolled in, obscuring their view and crawling up Oliver's skin, leaving a trail of goosebumps in its wake. The mist carried with it memories from across the timelines, as if this battleground, rather than love, was what resonated through the ages. In future timelines, Oliver favored the calculated tension of arena-style battles, where clever and strategic maneuvers could be truly appreciated. He was particularly fond of wielding fire as a tool of destruction, having pushed the boundaries of his imagination to its limits. Was the mist suggesting he apply some of that same strategic thinking here? It seemed to be sinking its teeth into him, sending a chill that penetrated his very bones, despite his distance from the water.

The wind carried a whisper through the air. "Féth Fíada!"— a phrase that pulled to the surface memories of his discussions with Elizabeth about the Tuatha Dé Danann. They had mostly transformed into faeries over time. Could they be lurking within the mist?

His foes were using the region's ancient magic against him. No matter. He had encountered their meddling before—being thrust through portals, enduring telepathic embolisms, and being scorched by ritual flames.

Suddenly, dozens of hares darted through the ranks of his men, their quick movements causing a stir. "If they bother you, catch them for your dinner," he instructed with a calm authority. "Carry on. Do not let them distract you."

Surveying the scene for his companions, Oliver sought Ruarc and Aodhán, who frequently calmed the men, maintaining order. How difficult could it be to capture a lady? They needed to target the steeple once more, as it still defiantly stood. At Oliver's command, a roaring cannon fire shattered the air, a thunderous blast that echoed across the misty landscape.

His next order called for a larger cannonball. The men responded with swift precision. A thunderous rumble coursed through the air, followed by an explosion that reverberated through the mist, sending up a towering plume of smoke and debris, a testament to the battle's fury.

The iron shot tore into the stone, carving a jagged breach in the spire's lower wall. Oliver was certain he'd heard a gasp from the defenders beyond. His pulse leapt with exhilaration.

He called for another hefty cannonball, straightening his shoulders in resolve. Raking his hand through his hair, he fixed his gaze on his target.

At this time, there were two main kinds of siege guns. Mortars lobbed powder-filled shells in a high arc that exploded with terrible force; cannons hurled solid iron balls to batter down masonry. The largest pieces in Ireland usually fired twelve or fourteen-pound shots—enough to dent Drogheda's walls, but not bring them down. Oliver, however, commanded far mightier beasts: demi-culverins, whole culverins, and cannon royals that fired rounds several times larger.

He ordered his gunners to fire without mercy until the steeple collapsed in ruin, then to wheel their pieces on the corner bastion of the city wall. His men would labor through the afternoon and into the evening, never pausing, until the stubborn tower—unbroken for centuries—lay in rubble. Sir Arthur Aston would soon discover the fatal mistake of refusing to surrender.

No great victory came without effort; this one would be won stone by stone. Oliver stood tall among his crews, demanding their respect. He was scaling yet another mountain of his own making, though fate still balanced precariously for and against him.

Was all this carnage destined to yield nothing, or had he at last broken free of history's cycle? A sudden vision struck him: a Neolithic monument, a coven, Elizabeth breaking a curse— with Claudia at her side.

So his true opponent would be her—his foe's heir—as fate had always decreed. Memories crashed over him amid the roar of cannon fire. How could he win over Claudia? Then it came to him: if Elizabeth could not be saved, he would pursue Alex instead.

Had his journeys through time changed him, or was he doomed to replay the same drama? What count this victory unless it broke the cycle once and for all?

He must convince Claudia that Alex held the key—and make her believe the idea was hers alone. He needed to plant a single seed: the notion that the dockworkers themselves possessed the power to end the bloodshed.

If he were to allow them to think they could stop the bombing, how could he do it successfully? He ordered those manning the cannon to take interval breaks but clued in his spies to keep vigilant watch.

But his men would need time to recover before they could storm Drogheda. True, Arthur would have his men shore up the walls during the break, but it would be far too little, far too late. Next, Arthur would dig trenches so the Irish could erect parapets for their musketeers, rendering the fallen steeple all but useless to Oliver. It would demand every last man though—exhausting them and leaving them open to counterattack.

Just as the Irish spirits had soared, the thunder of another cannon would shatter their hope. Under leaden skies and falling rubble, their resolve would crumble.

Here and there the wall was six feet thick, yet Arthur's men would still peer through the breach at the enemy's strong infantry. That opening would become Oliver's entry point—so why did he feel such dread?

Where were Ruarc and Aodhán? He'd left orders for them and now returned to camp. Once he retrieved Claudia, he could send his two closest friends to clear the debris and forge a path for his cavalry. A simple pulley and nets might suffice. Perhaps the townsfolk would bolt for it once the way was clear.

As he passed a row of tents, a whiff of rosewater drifted out alongside Lochlainn's voice. Instinctively, he ducked behind a canvas and listened.

It was their closeness that unnerved him. Lochlainn—a man he knew was a clone counter—seemed strangely intimate with Elizabeth. He watched them speak, felt a jolt of jealousy as Lochlainn offered her comfort. What if it wasn't Marie who had summoned him, but Elizabeth? And if so, why? Was her loyalty slipping after all they'd endured?

Worse still, Elizabeth moved with a lightness in Lochlainn's presence she had never shown Oliver. Her shoulders relaxed, her smile came easily, as if a weight had lifted. Oliver couldn't imagine her leaning on anyone else. She was everything he wanted—but did she feel the same? That radiant grin, the first since their child's death, was not for him.

No, he was losing control, letting his emotions consume him like a wildfire. Elizabeth frequently had to rein in the troops when his fury rendered him incapable. Her soothing presence was a balm, instilling confidence and calm among the ranks. She likely realized that Lochlainn, as Marie's clone counter, was essential to keep near for Oliver's sake.

Ruarc and Aodhán's voices cut sharply through the encampment, their footsteps heavy with urgency as they approached Oliver's tent. Oliver intercepted them with a steely gaze before they could enter. "Where is she?" he demanded, his voice a razor's edge, referring to the missing Claudia.

"We did exactly as you instructed and searched for Marie/Laura's daughter!" Aodhán retorted, his tone laced with frustration.

Hearing the commotion from outside, Marie swiftly conjured a powerful cloaking spell to ensure Claudia remained hidden from prying eyes.

"Fools! She's with Barnabus and Mary!" Oliver barked, his impatience boiling over.

"Your wife's family, Sir?" Ruarc questioned, bewilderment etched across his features.

"Yes, how else do you think she amassed such power?" Oliver snapped, his words biting.

"If you say so," Aodhán responded, skepticism hanging in the air.

Marie could only cling to the hope that her spell would hold strong, shielding Claudia from discovery.

But the next day, they still did not have Claudia, and his plans had truly been thrown off course!

"Why don't any of you have her daughter?" Oliver inquired sharply, his eyes narrowing at his assembled men. Silence met his question, causing his frustration to simmer just beneath the surface. With an exasperated sigh, he strode toward Marie, a sinister smirk stretching across his lips, like a predator toying with its prey.

"You know," he drawled, his voice dripping with mockery as he tucked a stray lock of hair behind Marie's ear, causing her to recoil in disgust, "my soldiers slept well last night, better than they ever have. Did you have anything to do with that?"

"Why would I tell you if I did?" Marie retorted, her voice steady despite the fear flickering in her eyes.

Without a moment's hesitation, Oliver turned sharply on his heel and marched over to Aodhán, delivering a swift punch to his jaw. The impact was brutal, sending Aodhán stumbling to the ground, his hand flying to his mouth as he glared up at Oliver with a mixture of pain and defiance.

"That was uncalled for," Ruarc barked, his voice boiling with rage, his fists clenched at his sides.

"You want to be next?" Oliver taunted, his tone dripping with malice.

"Why are you so cruel?" Ruarc seethed, his voice barely containing his anger.

Oliver raised his pistol, leveling it directly at Ruarc. His heart hammered in his chest, each beat echoing loudly in his ears. Suddenly, a swift movement caught his attention, and before he could react, Lochlainn had deftly removed the pistol from his grip with a speed that was almost inhuman.

"What do you think you're doing?" Oliver demanded, his voice edged with disbelief as he turned to Lochlainn. He reached for his sword, but Lochlainn was quicker, disarming him with the same fluid motion.

"I'm just keeping you from doing unnecessary harm, Sir," Lochlainn said calmly, his voice steady and unyielding.

"Fine, have it your way," Oliver spat, resentment dripping from his words. "Ruarc, escort my wife so that she's standing next to Laura."

Ruarc stood frozen, his mind racing. Only the sound of Oliver's impatient stomping broke his paralysis, prompting him to flinch and hurry toward Elizabeth.

"Why are you involving Elizabeth in this?" Lochlainn demanded, his voice firm and questioning.

"What's it to you?" Oliver snapped, irritation flashing in his eyes.

The air within the tent was tense and suffocating, a heavy silence draped over the occupants like a shroud. Aodhán slowly rose to his feet, still massaging his bruised jaw, while Lochlainn stood resolute, pistol and sword securely in hand. Marie shifted her feet uneasily, her gaze darting between the men.

Finally, Ruarc guided Elizabeth next to Marie/Laura, her expression one of confusion and distress.

"What's going on?" Elizabeth asked, her voice tinged with bewilderment. "Why do you have Laura chained to a stake?"

"Dear, this is for you," Oliver claimed, his words a twisted mockery of affection.

"I never asked for this," Elizabeth replied, her voice firm and filled with quiet defiance.

"You've put an end to the curse, but there's more," Oliver said, his voice heavy with unspoken burdens. "Maybe you should have a seat." He gently pulled out a sturdy wooden chair from the table for her, its legs scraping softly against the dirt floor.

"I don't understand how that makes any of this necessary," Elizabeth declared, her brow furrowed in confusion and defiance.

"It's for our children," Oliver pleaded, his eyes softening with earnest emotion. "You and them are always very much in my heart."

Elizabeth exhaled deeply, the weight of her husband's caring words pressing upon her resolve. "My life is but half a life in your absence," she admitted, her voice tinged with longing.

And there it was, the romance that had sparked it all—a love that, despite hardships and doomed destinies, transcended everything, perhaps even to a fault.

"I have Laura here in order to reincarnate ourselves so that we may love each other for an eternity," Oliver revealed, his voice steady but filled with an almost desperate hope.

Neither Aodhán, Ruarc, nor Lochlainn showed any signs of surprise at his declaration. Elizabeth, on the other hand, looked as if the ground had shifted beneath her feet, her eyes wide with shock.

"You have the wrong woman," Elizabeth said, exasperation threading through her voice like a taut string.

"What do you mean?" Oliver asked, his brow creasing with confusion.

"Mary's the only one in town with the power to carry out such a task," Elizabeth stated with unwavering confidence.

"How do you know Laura does not hold the same power?" Oliver questioned.

"Mary's my sister," Elizabeth explained, her voice steady and sure. "Plus, I had her reincarnate our lost child."

"You what?" Oliver asked, his voice rising in disbelief.

"I…" Elizabeth began, her words faltering.

"No, I heard you," Oliver barked, his mind reeling. "I'm just trying to wrap my brain around it. You did that before the curse was lifted, meaning it will carry forward!"

Elizabeth's breath caught in her throat, leading to a coughing fit that doubled her over. Oliver's expression shifted to one of immediate concern, his eyes scanning her with worry.

At that moment, a soldier marched into the tent, his boots clomping against the ground. "Sir, there's something wrong with the cannons," he reported, his voice urgent.

"What is it?" Oliver asked sharply, as Lochlainn handed him back his sword and pistol, their metallic surfaces gleaming under the dim light.

"The touchholes, Sir," the soldier explained. "Someone's jammed them!"

"All of them?" Oliver's voice was a mix of disbelief and anger as he stormed out of the tent, Aodhán and Ruarc trailing him closely. The pair had to maintain pretenses lest they be branded as deserters.

Lochlainn hesitated at the tent entrance. "Will you be all right?" he asked, concern etching his features.

Elizabeth nodded, her face pale but resolute.

As soon as he left, Marie rose quietly and approached Elizabeth, her movements gentle. She handed over a small bottle of cough medicine, its glass cool and smooth to the touch. "Here, take this to stop those fits you've been having," she offered kindly.

Elizabeth accepted the bottle, its contents sloshing softly as she tucked it into her pocket for safekeeping.

Oliver stormed through the battery courtyard and halted beside the line of cannons. Barbed spikes crisscrossed their touchholes, and crude solder seals glistened like dark scars in the morning light. His jaw clenched so tight his teeth ached. Fixing them would take days—days he did not have if he meant to bring down the bastion looming over Drogheda. He could almost taste the acrid smoke that should have curled over the walls and smothered that ancient tower—one that had mocked every siege for a century—until its stones gave way and the whole edifice collapsed in ruin. Now, that triumph was slipping from his grasp.

"Check the second arms and ammunitions tent," he barked, voice raw.

His captains scattered. There were a handful of cannons stored there, some already prepped but idle. It would cost precious hours, yet they were all he had. His enemy, Laura, was complicating matters—stalling, maneuvering. Oliver's gut knotted with frustration.

He grabbed Ruarc's sleeve. "Go into town—fetch Mary. Now."

Ruarc's face went pale at the name, but he nodded and vanished into the shadows of the camp. Oliver watched him go, pulse hammering in his temples.

Sweat dripped from the men's brows despite the cool weather as they hauled the untampered cannons out and moved the blocked ones away. Oliver's heart pounded as frustration grew within him. He would not let this hold him back from his mission. Some of his men simply made a path, others breathed hard while pulling the heavy-duty wheeled gun carriages, and the rest waited on the ships to use ropes for lifting.

All of the preparation to place the cannons just right was for not and had to be redone. Oliver was bloody pissed with the additional required effort. Once in place, the wheels would be removed from the carriages to prevent rolling. He barked orders for his men to hurry despite their clear fatigue as the thought of being delayed by hours was maddening.

At last, the replacement guns boomed against the walls. But the toil had been monstrous, the delay intolerable—and still Ruarc had not returned. Oliver's patience snapped. His boots crunched over the ground as he stalked the lines into the fading day. Every breath flared with fury.

Under cover of darkness, Sir Arthur Aston had had his men repair yesterday's havoc—resetting slabs of stone, packing fresh mortar into shattered seams. They'd dug trenches, heaped dirt into sturdy parapets for musketeers to take cover. Oliver halted at the sight, blood roaring through his ears.

He yanked Aodhán aside, eyes blazing like coals. "Gather the best assassins you can find. Kill Mary, Barnabus, Claudia, Alex. All of them. Let nothing stand in your way."

Aodhán's throat bobbed as he swallowed. "Sir … we need Mary to reincarnate."

Oliver's laugh was a rasping snarl. Every muscle in his body throbbed with the weight of his wrath. "They know too much, and we have Laura. They no longer serve me. Slit their throats before they can slip through death's door and come back to haunt us. If they plan to rob me of victory, I'll take everything from them."

A cold fire ignited in his chest, spreading so rapidly he felt as though his skin might catch aflame. History had twisted and writhed beneath his command time and again, despite every crusade for change. He would not see this victory stolen.

When the cannons finally shattered the outer wall in two ominous breaches, Oliver's rage erupted in a scream he didn't know he'd held. Victory shimmered on the horizon. He remembered—another timeline, the guards he'd unleashed on his foes there, the merciless slaughter he'd ordered while his mind frayed at the edges of sanity.

He yanked a steel helm from a nearby soldier and strapped it on with a barbaric grin. "Charge!" he roared, and plunged headlong into the assault, every beat of his heart a pulse of unquenchable fury.

At the breach, they clawed their way over the mound of shattered stone. A salvo of musketeers thundered, ripping through flesh and bone, dropping dozens of his men like butchered cattle. Screams pierced the air—raw, animal sounds that cut through gunsmoke. Men writhed impaled on pikes, their lifeblood gushing onto the rubble while others fled in terror.

Oliver charged forward, his heart hammering against his ribs. "FORWARD!" he bellowed, spittle flying from his lips. At the other breach, his cannons roared, belching half-pound iron death into the enemy cavalry. Men swarmed behind him like a tide of vengeance.

The musketeers faltered, eyes wide with panic as Oliver's horde descended upon them. Drogheda men and horses thrashed in their death throes, intestines spilling onto the cobblestones. Blood splattered Oliver's face, metallic on his tongue.

"PUSH ON!" he screamed, sword raised high. The Drogheda forces broke, fleeing in blind terror. His men surged beyond the wall, howling as they overtook the parapets. Musketeers scrambled backward, fumbling to reload weapons they'd never fire again.

His men poured across the drawbridge, boots thundering on wood. Fierce exhilaration coursed through Oliver's veins like fire. They flooded the main street, a tidal wave of steel and fury.

They fell upon enemy soldiers with inhuman shrieks, hacking and stabbing before swords could clear scabbards. The city became a cacophony of splintering bone, screams, and death rattles.

His cavalry thundered behind, trampling the fallen. Drogheda was his—a slaughterhouse victory. Mangled corpses carpeted the streets, some still twitching.

"Break Drogheda and we break all of Ireland!" Oliver roared, blood-flecked spittle flying. "LET NONE ESCAPE! NO QUARTER! DO YOU UNDERSTAND?"

Battles erupted everywhere as the enemy scattered like rats. Only Oliver's men moved with deadly purpose. The city had never imagined their walls would crumble.

A spy appeared, breathless: "Citizens flee through the gates!" The news ignited Oliver's blood to boiling rage. Mary—escaping? The thought alone made him grip his sword until his knuckles whitened. Not while he still drew breath.

As if the very fate of his army depended on his mood, they wavered under uncertainty. Musket balls tore through the air, finding their targets with deadly precision and felling some of his men. Aston's second in command seized the moment, rallying his forces with renewed clarity. The enemy was clawing back territories Oliver believed were firmly in his grip.

Instead of unwavering obedience, he witnessed a young officer and his company foolishly accept surrender when they should have been merciless, cutting down their foes without hesitation. His heart sank further as he observed the enemy gaining ground in a fierce clash near the church.

Desperation clawed at him; he had to secure the gates. He rallied some infantry, determined to set a guard that would permit no escapes. But when he reached the gate, the wide street leading to it was far from deserted. A formidable assembly of Irish infantry stood ready.

Pikemen and musketeers swiftly fell into battle formation. There were scores, perhaps a hundred men, and from a side street, Irish cavalry surged forward, forming a protective barrier before the troops.

Oliver's heart pounded as he glanced back. Only twenty men stood with him, mounted and armed but heavily outnumbered. He roared for reinforcements, determined to muster courage against overwhelming odds. At least, he was flanked by seasoned veterans, warriors forged in the crucible of battle.

He could not permit any to escape. Just then, the heavens seemed to conspire in his favor, as the clouds split apart, casting a blinding glare into the enemy's eyes. In that moment of clarity, where the shadows returned, Oliver saw his objective. With a fierce cry, he thrust his sword into the air and bellowed, "Charge!"

CHAPTER SEVENTEEN – CLAUDIA

"May the road rise up to meet you, may the wind be always at
your back, may the sunshine warm upon your face…"
(An Irish Blessing)

Alex and I traipse to the first tent we'd stopped by, the canvas flapping like nervous birds in the dawn breeze. We grab a cloak each—rough-spun wool that smells of woodsmoke and sweat. I search for my mother, but she's still nowhere to be seen. It pains me to leave without her, but we're no good to her if we're caught. Sneaking our way out of camp isn't too difficult since most of the men are barely awake, their bleary eyes fixed on morning cook fires or their own trembling hands. Meeting up with the rest of the crew, we set back out in boats, across the water to our side, oars dipping silently into the mist-shrouded lake.

"What happened to you?" Conor asks Alex, his face pinched with concern.

"Got stabbed." Alex shrugs, but the movement causes him to wince, a thin line of crimson seeping through his bandages.

"Yeah, you're not going to be much help in the battle," Conor exclaims, his voice carrying over the gentle lapping of water against the wooden hull.

"You got the cannons," Alex says, his voice strained but steady. "There's not going to be a battle."

Conor raps his knuckles against the weathered oak of the boat, the hollow sound echoing across the water. A local tradition to prevent evil spirits from listening in when there's a boast. The knock is to prevent the reversal of fortune, like closing a door on fate's ears.

"What's this about no battle?" Liam asks, his hair catching the first rays of sunlight, and Conor knocks again, harder this time.

"Alex was stabbed in camp, and Conor said he wouldn't be much help in a battle," I say, my fingers tracing the damp edge of the boat. "Alex was just stating it might not be necessary."

"'Might' would be the key word there, Claudia," Rí says, his eyes scanning the horizon like a hawk.

With his words, we turn to the battlements to see what we're up against, masts with sails rising like gray teeth against the pale morning sky.

"They have more cannons?" I ask as panic creeps up my throat, cold as ice water. If that's the case, did we only delay the inevitable?

"We better get into position," Conor says, checking the powder horn at his belt for the third time.

"I'll take Alex to be healed," I respond, supporting his weight against my shoulder. "Should we send any messages along the way?"

"Tell any pretty lady you see that I love them," Liam exclaims, a rakish grin splitting his face despite the circumstances. He's to stand back and be a musketeer given that he's still recovering, wrapped in linen bandages, so it's not likely he'll be in as much danger as Rí and Conor, but I shouldn't be surprised with his request. He'll find any reason to talk to a pretty lady, even with death looming.

"Tell our friends and family to be ready to leave through the northwest gate just in case," Rí says, his voice like gravel, which is a sobering thought that settles in my stomach like lead.

Conor knocks on wood again, his knuckles white with the force. "Let's give them hell, boys."

A battle cry rings out on our side of the water, a hundred voices becoming one terrible roar. Fear squeezes my chest, and my heart aches at the thought of leaving them to possibly die, these men who have become my family. Alex's jaw clenches, the muscle twitching beneath his stubbled skin, and I can see how difficult it is for him to leave too, to abandon his brothers to fate.

He's no use to them until he's healed. I silently cast a small protection spell for Alex's crew, my lips forming the ancient words as my fingers trace invisible sigils in the air, adding that their aim be sure and true, that their courage never falter, that they return with beating hearts.

"Claudia," Conor calls, his voice sharp against the crackle of distant gunfire. He points down the muddy trail. "Róis's cottage is closer than Mary's—and her hands hold more power for healing."

I exchange a glance with Alex. He shrugs; I nod. "Thank you." Together, we step away, boots squelching in the wet earth.

As we trudge beneath dripping branches, Alex's voice cuts through the hush. "What did you actually see back at camp when you brushed against that counter?"

I press my lips together, forcing back a shiver. "Lochlainn was carried here by Elizabeth, not Cromwell. And if Cromwell's magic truly fused two souls into one body...he can't cycle back again."

He lets out a soft whistle. "Well, that sounds like a win."

I shrug, kicking at a bog-soaked root. "Sure—but I was hoping for...something more climactic. Cromwell's twisted games haunted me for lifetimes. I even ended him once— maybe I owe myself some peace this time."

The echoes of distant explosions grow faint as the dwelling's thatch roof pokes through the trees. Moss climbs the hazel frame, and the air smells of damp wood and wildflowers. Alex halts, scanning the treeline. "It feels wrong, leaving Conor and the others out there to fight."

I squeeze his hand. His knuckles go white, and he glances away. "I'm willing to bet Étaín's already brewing a distraction—she and Conor might bark loud, but they're soft at heart. No doubt she's concocting something to blind Cromwell's forces."

A ghost of a smile flickers on his lips. I wish I could bear him against my chest, carry him the rest of the way.

As we round the corner, Neasa steps away from the doorway toward us, her gray hair pinned back with hawthorn sprigs. "I don't know how I knew, but I expected you two." She spreads her arms. "Come in."

Alex dips his head. "Sorry to be a bother… think you could help with this?" He lifts his tunic to reveal a blood-darkened bandage across his ribs.

Neasa's brow furrows. "What happened, love?"

"We snuck into the enemy camp for Laura," he confesses, his voice tight, "and I ended up with a blade instead."

Inside, the cottage feels snug—warmed by a crackling hearth. Onóra gestures to a low wooden stool beside a bubbling earthenware pot. Steam scented with lavender and something metallic curls toward the rafters.

Étaín, her cheeks ruddy from the firelight, hovers by a shelf of jars. "How's my brave soldier?" she asks Alex, her tone gentle beneath fierce eyes.

He leans forward. "They managed to block most of the cannon touchholes—but not all."

"Every shield matters," she murmurs.

Róis steps closer, robes swishing over the stone floor. I unwind Alex's bandage just enough for her fingertips to brush the raw skin. She presses gloved fingers to the wound's edge, brow knitted in concentration. "Could you heal this?" Alex's jaw tightens. "I hate being away from the front lines."

Étaín exchanges a glance with Onóra, then nods. "He'll be back on his feet soon. Conor needs every ally he can get."

My heart twists at the thought of Alex rejoining the fray. My chest burns. I bite my lip, steadying myself. "What can I do?"

Róis turns, voice softening. "Could you gather white rosa canina rosehips from the hawthorn grove outside?"

I hurry past the window, nestling through damp grass until I'm surrounded by gnarly hawthorn trunks. Clusters of bright orange hips shine among thorny branches. I pluck them, fingers prickled by barbs, then race back inside.

Neasa holds out her hand, palm up. I press the rosehips into her palm. When our skin meets, a warm pulse drifts between us—no vision, but a message of trust. Her gentle smile confirms what I've only dared whisper: she's known about time travel, about us, since day one.

We bow our heads toward the old hawthorn tree beyond the window—silent thanks for its shelter and strength. Onóra returns with a chipped mug brimming with pale blue water. "Laura brewed this the moment she arrived," she says, setting it beside the pot. The healing begins.

"Airmid, Goddess of Healing, daughter of Dian Cecht, we call upon your grace," we intone in unison, breath steaming in the cool air. The firelight flickers against the walls as our voices rise. "You who know the language of leaves and streams, guide this water toward restoration. Grant us compassion, that we may channel your gift of healing."

"Blessed be," I whisper, voice soft but steady.

I unlace Alex's blood-smudged bandages, revealing the stab wound in his side. The stitches tore during our escape. Onóra lifts the chipped mug brimming with pale blue water. She drizzles the cool liquid over the wound. A hiss of relief escapes him as the water sluices away blood.

Róis kneels beside us, fingers stained deep rose as she crushes plump rosehips between her palms. Viscous scarlet droplets bead on Alex's flesh, searing warmth radiating inward. The flesh knits so quickly that I can almost feel the sinew weaving itself back together. Róis presses a fresh linen square to the cut, her brow furrowed in concentration. I help wrap him snugly, the crisp cloth drawing away the last traces of moisture.

Alex exhales, tension leaving his shoulders. The flicker of pain remains in his eyes, but his lips curve into a faint, grateful smile.

Étaín steps forward, voice ringing like the chime of a distant bell. "Now, we turn our art toward disarraying the enemy."

Neasa props her hand on a carved oak table. "Their commander wields cunning magic himself—he's unnaturally precise for a fairly green leader."

Alex frowns. "How do you know?"

Neasa's lips curve. "First, his ranks maneuver in perfect synchrony despite such raw command. Second," she leans closer, voice low, "he's wed to someone from our sister coven in town."

My heart lurches. I taste iron on my tongue. My aunt's face—her gentle smile—crowds my thoughts. Did she teach him these tactics? Did she foresee the river of blood this siege would spill? Doubt coils around my ribs, icy and relentless.

Étaín's soft clap pulls me back. She holds a clay cauldron thick with a frothy brew of vervain, foxglove, and wolf's-bane petals. "We'll cast a piseóg," she explains, sweeping her hand over a scatter of bones and feathers. "First, stir clockwise, envisioning all the luck and success that favors them. Then reverse our motion and reclaim that fortune."

We each dip a carved blackthorn stick into the bubbling mix in the cauldron. I close my eyes, picturing the enemy's banners snapping in the wind, their swords flashing victory. My stir draws ribbons of steam into a slender column that disappears through the smoke hole overhead. Then we turn our wrists, digging deep into the brew, anchoring our own hopes—victory, safety, triumph. The cauldron gurgles its assent.

"That should do it," Onóra says, tapping the stick against the rim, sending a final puff of mist upward.

Étaín lays a hand on Alex's shoulder. "Rest before you return to Conor's side. Even good magic drains you."

"Thank you," Alex murmurs, voice huskier than before.

We tread to the cave under a sky fat with plumes of battle smoke. The stone of the cavern feels comforting, but the path into the cave now seems charged—final. Every loose stone, every whisper of wind through bracken feels like a reminder of what waits. I glance at Alex's profile—strong jaw, hair damp with dew—and my chest tightens.

Inside the cavern's mouth, I lean into him, pressing along the uninjured side so our bodies fit like pieces in a puzzle. The firelight glints on rough stone, but all I see is the curve of his shoulder, the warmth he radiates. I lift my face to his and claim his lips with all the yearning I've kept buried. His stubble grazes my cheek, sharp and grounding, and I taste peppermint oil lingering on his breath.

His arm wraps around my waist, pulling me flush against the firm ridges of muscle I can now trace beneath his shirt. He kisses me back with an urgency that echoes mine: hungry, unrestrained. My fingers find his hair at the nape. His palm slides from my hip to cradle my cheek, thumb brushing across my pulse point.

Between heated kisses, I whisper, "I love you." My voice is a confession and a vow.

He stills, eyes sparkling in the firelight. Then his fingers curl into the back of my dress, and he answers against my mouth, "I love you more."

My pulse flutters, body alight. I press one hand to his chest, feeling the thrumming beat beneath my palm. He leans in, forehead to temple, and our breath mingles. His lips find mine again, deeper, fiercer—two flames colliding until the world narrows to heat, to the steady drum of his heart, to the promise we share in every kiss.

"Claudia?" My mother interrupts us. She's safe! She escaped!

Alex pulls away and smooths his hair. "Glad to see you're free, Marie," he says to her.

"How did you sneak out of the tent?" I ask.

"It's a long story," she responds. "And we don't have time."

"What do you mean?" I ask. "What are you talking about?"

"Are you joining Étaín to help with the battle?" Alex inquires.

"No, listen," Mother's voice trembles with a mixture of frustration and dread as we stand in the cavern. Flickering torchlight dances across her stern features. "Bringing you into this timeline was a mistake. I need to be certain Mary performs the reincarnation spell even if Elizabeth doesn't collapse, and I can't focus on that if I'm worried about you."

A cold wind snakes through the tunnel. I swallow hard, my heart pounding. "But there's still so much to do." My words echo off the rough stone walls.

Alex steps closer, shoulders squared. "We want to help with the battle," he says, his voice firm but edged with uncertainty.

I glance between them. "What if something goes wrong, and you can't reach Mary in time? I thought it would be disastrous if she recognized you. I'm part of Mary's coven now—surely, I should be the one persuading her."

Mother inhales sharply, as if tasting my words. "With the knowledge Mary possesses, she'll understand," she insists. Her eyes flare. "Besides, I—my past self—has already performed a reincarnation spell in this lifetime."

I blink, startled. "Oh—who?"

Her lips tighten. "Elizabeth's lost child," she blurts, voice quick as though the faster she speaks, the less lasting the revelation.

My breath hitches. "That...explains so much across the timelines." My mind races, connecting half-remembered moments. "But why didn't Elizabeth bring her child back to life?"

Shock spreads across Mother's face, casting her gentle features into sharp relief. "What do you know about resurrection?" she demands, pacing the uneven ground.

I stiffen. "I didn't want Hugh's child left without a father. I've seen how deeply that wound cuts."

Alex's jaw drops, and I feel the cavern grow colder still. Mother stops, her forehead creased. "Tell me exactly what you did," she murmurs, almost to herself.

So I recount the night Elizabeth and I gathered the sacred items—the goose eggshell, the dirt where death occurred, the personal item of the fallen—and called upon the Goddess Morrigan beneath the moon. Alex's eyes widen while Mother's pacing grows frantic.

"And Elizabeth never warned you of the ill effects that accompany such formidable magic?" Mother's voice is quiet but charged.

My pulse races. "No. I meant to ask you—did Hugh survive in the first timeline?"

A thoughtful pause. Then Mother's expression shifts, as understanding dawns. "Yes. Hugh returned, miraculously, in the original sequence. But the battle loomed, and my focus was torn apart."

Alex's brows knit together in concern. "What kind of ill effects are we talking about?"

Mother's gaze turns distant, haunted by memories. "Perhaps that burden killed Elizabeth back then—casting the spell alone, absorbing every ounce of grief and regret."

My stomach drops. "So now I share that burden with her?"

Alex's voice snaps. "No! How do we stop it?"

Mother's shoulders slump. She exhales, the sound hollow. "Return to the 1920s. The temporal shift will shield you from the backlash."

I press my hand to my throat, remembering Elizabeth's fragile cough. "But Elizabeth's the only one showing symptoms—"

"I'd rather not take the risk," Alex interrupts softly, wrapping his arms around me. His warmth is a comfort in this chill chamber. "I've already been stabbed here once. Let's go home."

Moments later, we're stepping out of the cave into the forest. The air is damp and earthy, heavy with the scent of moss. I gather fallen oak in one hand, maple leaves in the other, recalling my original purpose: protect Alex. I never imagined these woods would host counters or that he'd taste blood here. My stomach lurches at the thought of the coming carnage.

Alex and I stand in a small clearing, the sky above remarkably blue. I set the oak leaves alight, pale smoke curling upward in a protective ring. Mother places maple leaves in her brazier, the resinous scent mingling with the oak. We chant low words of travel and protection. Familiar spells slip from my lips, but I pray with all my heart that we'll never need their power again.

Once we intone the word 'Awen' three times, I lock eyes with Mother and whisper, "Until we meet again, Awen." With those words, Alex and I dissolve into thin air. We find ourselves enveloped by a whirlwind of Drogheda's vibrant scenes, spinning around us so swiftly that a wave of nausea threatens to overwhelm me.

A powerful hum pulsates between us, echoing the final words spoken. The sharp scent of charred oak invades my nostrils, while wisps of smoke curl lazily above us. My body is caught in a tumultuous dance, twisting and turning without restraint.

I clutch Alex's hand tightly, and he enfolds me in a warm embrace, anchoring me to reality and instilling a profound sense of wholeness. My spirit steadies, and just as swiftly, we arrive in the sun-dappled yard of Olinda. As our eyes connect, a surge of warmth blooms in my chest.

"Wow, I don't know if I could ever get used to that feeling," Alex exclaims, his voice filled with awe.

We make our way around to the welcoming door and knock. When Olinda opens it, surprise softens her features as she clasps her hands to her mouth. A single tear glides down her cheek before she envelops us both in a heartfelt embrace. The gentle hum of voices drifts out from the dining room, beckoning us.

Everyone is gathered here. Alex first embraces his ma and little brother, Wendell, who clings sleepily to him. Relief washes over his ma's face at the sight of him. He then turns to greet his friends—Frank, James, and Thomas—with hearty slaps on the back and familiar side hugs. It dawns on me how much his friends here echo his crew in Ireland—Rí, Conor, and Liam.

Florian and Kiersten rush to join me, and we all share a collective hug, the contact both comforting and invigorating. Lina hesitates for a moment, disbelief etched on her face. "You're really here?" she asks, her voice tinged with wonder. I pull her into our welcoming embrace, the warmth of my dear friends surrounding me like a soft blanket.

Nelly and Olinda approach our group tentatively. "Marie's not with you?" Nelly inquires, a flicker of anxiety shadowing her eyes.

"No, but she shouldn't be but a day behind," I reassure her, hoping fervently that my words hold true.

"We were just sitting down for supper," Olinda says, her voice inviting. "Please, join us."

As we gather around the table, a wave of déjà vu washes over me, a familiar sensation I can't quite place. Once Alex's ma and Wendell finish their meal, they bid us goodbye, with Wendell half asleep, his head lolling adorably. I feel a deep sense of contentment, grateful to be in a place so serene and soothing.

"I do love this dress style," Florian exclaims, her eyes twinkling with admiration as she runs her fingers over the fabric. "Can I borrow it sometime?"

"Of course," I reply warmly, her passion for fashion painting a smile across my face.

"Was there a feminist movement present?" Kiersten inquires, her voice carrying a tone of curiosity.

"We were fighting to return to Behron Law, which embraced female leadership and the freedom to love whom you wish, among many other great things," I explain, recalling the fervent energy of the past.

"Oh, wonderful, so it was very similar to here," Lina remarks, her eyes widening with interest.

"What?" I ask, a flicker of surprise in my voice. "We were just fighting for the right to vote before I left."

"That's odd," Florian muses before leaning in to kiss Kiersten, a gentle gesture of affection. "I don't remember that at all."

"Yeah," Kiersten agrees, nodding. "Our president, Soledad Chacon, is a woman."

I turn to Alex, my mind racing with the implications. "We changed things!"

"I guess so," he responds with a grin, his eyes shimmering with pride, "for the better, it seems."

"I wonder if Ireland was able to return to her roots too," I say, my thoughts swirling with the tantalizing possibilities.

"Wait," Alex interjects, glancing at his friends with raised eyebrows. "What about prohibition?"

"What?" Thomas replies, confusion etched on his face. "No, no laws on alcohol here in Missouri."

"But we…" Alex gestures between himself and his friends. "We still met and knew each other. That didn't change."

"That will never change!" James declares with conviction.

Frank pulls Alex into a side hug, a bond of camaraderie evident. "Never!"

"Wow, this is all a lot to take in," Nelly admits, her voice tinged with awe.

"Why don't I bring out some dessert?" Olinda suggests, her offer a welcome distraction.

As we indulge in sweet treats, our conversation shifts to Drogheda in 1649, and everyone listens intently, perched at the edge of their seats. Nelly and Olinda nearly take notes as we delve into the mysteries of magic. When I describe the festival, Florian nearly topples her chair in excitement. Alex's friends eagerly inquire about taverns and weapons, their eyes alight with curiosity.

It's heartwarming to see the broad smiles encircling the table. I feel a sense of belonging, yet there's an emptiness, a longing for familiar faces. I miss Barnabus and Mary, as well as Elizabeth. I think Fidelma and Líadan would find kindred spirits in Kiersten and Florian. As I glance at Alex, I wonder if he shares these thoughts.

But the absence of my mother casts a shadow over the gathering. I hope she's safe and will join us soon.

"Sorry, I'm late," a familiar voice echoes through the air, gentle yet distinct. Everyone turns toward the front door, so I follow, and who I see knocks the wind out of me—Anna.

CHAPTER EIGHTEEN – ALEXANDER

"May your thoughts be as glad as the shamrocks.

May your heart be as light as a song.

May each day bring you bright, happy hours

That stay with you all the year long."

(An Irish Blessing)

The tension in the room eased like a slow exhale as the initial shock of seeing Anna faded. Claudia rushed forward, wrapping her arms around Anna's slender frame, but Anna's body stiffened beneath the embrace, her arms hanging awkwardly at her sides.

"What..." Claudia pulled back, her brow furrowed, eyes searching Anna's face. "Do you remember?"

"Oh, honey, I remember you," Anna said, tucking a strand of her mahogany hair behind her ear. "I just still can't believe everything that's occurred. Plus, it's disorienting remembering what happened before you left."

"Yeah," Nelly added, leaning against the weathered oak table. "The rest of us don't recall what happened before you time traveled."

"Gee," I said, shoving my hands into my pockets. "So why do you guys think we traveled?"

"Historical research, of course," Olinda said, but a mischievous smirk spread across her face, crinkling the corners of her eyes.

"You're messing with us?" I asked, my voice rising with disbelief.

"Oh, the no prohibition thing is no joke," Thomas said, his deep voice resonating in the cramped room. "But we remember prohibition before you left."

"Do you know how surreal it was to wake up, go to work, and see the alcohol on full display?" Kiersten asked, her eyes wide. "Everyone looked at me like I'd lost my mind when I yelled and hid a bottle of whiskey."

"I wonder what we changed in 1649 that caused the change here?" Claudia asked, her fingers nervously playing with the frayed edge of her pouch.

"What do the history books say about the siege now?" I asked, glancing around at the familiar yet somehow different faces of my friends.

"That's what's interesting." Olinda rose from her chair, the wooden legs scraping against the floor. She crossed to a dusty bookshelf and pulled out a leather-bound tome. "The pages were blank last I checked." She handed it to me, the weight of it substantial in my hands.

Claudia peered over my shoulder, her breath warm against my neck. "It's like the book is waiting. I feel its pain."

"So, what happened while you were there?" Lina asked, her eyes intense with curiosity.

Claudia described meeting her parents and aunt—or rather, their past lives' souls—her voice growing soft with emotion. Thankfully everyone, including Anna, remembered reincarnation, nodding along with understanding.

I recounted meeting my crew, the salt air and rough planks of the dock still vivid in my memory, and preparing for battle with hearts pounding and hands calloused. Then, I detailed how we blocked the cannons and sabotaged the enemy's supplies, the taste of victory bitter with the knowledge of what possibly was still to come.

"Maybe that's why the pages are blank," Florian offered, her lanky frame hunched forward in thought.

We all fell silent, the only sound the ticking of the antique clock on the mantel.

"But why are they blank?" Frank asked, running a hand through his hair. "If the battle was stopped."

"Because they had backup cannons when we had to leave," Claudia said, her voice barely above a whisper. "That's part of the reason Mother stayed."

"What, does she have a secret weapon or something?" James asked skeptically.

Nelly's lips curved into a conspiratorial grin, and Olinda's eyes sparkled in reply—so brightly that James's eyebrows shot up toward his hairline.

"Why did you have to come back?" Anna's voice trembled as she folded her arms across her chest, shoulders rising in a fragile barrier.

I leaned forward, fingertips tapping on the polished oak table. "Claudia resurrected someone alongside Elizabeth— well, the version of you from long ago, Anna. She had to return here to counteract the backlash of that spell."

Anna's hands flew to her mouth. "Oh, no... I'm sorry." She swallowed, then added with a brittle laugh, "It's happening again, isn't it? Elizabeth's sick."

Claudia laid a gentle hand on Anna's wrist. Her tone was calm, almost soothing. "It's all right. Bringing Hugh back was my idea."

Anna lifted her chin, pride flaring across her pale face. "Perhaps we're more alike than I realized. After losing my child centuries ago, I scoured every grimoire for a resurrection incantation—and finally succeeded."

I rubbed my thumb over a carved knot in the tabletop. "Has there been any hint of foul magic since then? Is Kris still behind bars?"

Anna shook her head. "I sense my husband's presence lingering... but nothing overtly malicious."

Claudia's gaze brightened. "That means the reincarnation took hold—that's a good sign."

Anna's brow furrowed. "Maybe," she whispered, uncertainty quivering in her tone.

Olinda cleared her throat and stretched. "Lovely catching up, truly—but I think everyone's ready to call it a night."

Kiersten leaned forward. "You didn't happen across any get-rich-quick secrets during your travel, did you? Because I'd kill to skip work tomorrow."

James thumped the table with a grin. "Yeah—some instant fortune would be nice."

Florian laughed and began describing the couture runway she'd launch if only she had the capital, spinning in her chair as though the spotlights were already on her. Frank and Thomas leaned in to debate possible investments, their voices rising. Before I knew it, the fire in the hearth had burned low, and the room felt too quiet, too still—yet it had only taken an hour or so for us to slip back into old rhythms, as if three hundred years of time had been nothing more than a blink.

Outside, the lantern-lit street was empty except for our footfalls on the brick road. Claudia tugged at her coat collar and glanced behind her, the lamplight dancing across her anxious features. "My mother might have something at home to show us her condition," she murmured. I sensed her guilt—she'd hated leaving history half–written—but relief outweighed it. She'd taken a bullet for me before we hopped eras; if someone tried to stab me again in Ireland, she'd step in without a second thought.

When we reached Marie's door, my breath caught in my throat. The entrance stood wide as if yanked from its hinges; porcelain shards from a once–elegant vase lay scattered across the threshold, petals of ceramic mingling with splinters of mahogany. Inside, chairs lay overturned, velvet cushions ripped open on the floor.

"Is anything missing?" I asked, voice tight as I leaned over a toppled bookshelf.

"I don't know," Claudia whispered, her eyes darting from one chaotic corner to the next. I straightened a lamp and set a heavy chaise upright, the scrape of legs on stone herringbone like a warning.

I stooped to lift the fallen tome—its leather cover cracked, a faint musty scent drifting up—when something crimson flashed on the floor. My fingers froze, heart stuttering. Silk. I knelt, brushing away debris to reveal a slender tie... the very one Kris had filched from Claudia what seemed like a lifetime ago. Curling it around my palm, I stood and called over my shoulder, "Claudia, look—Kris was here." Her breath hitched; she scanned the dim hallway.

"Do you think he's still inside?" she whispered, eyes darting toward the door.

"I doubt it," I said, voice steady but cautious. "Still, let's be certain."

She squared her shoulders. "I'm coming with you."

Her hand slipped into mine, cool skin against my own. The house lay silent—only our footsteps echoed as we swept through narrow rooms. I held back a surge of nerves, guiding her past tapestries, into the parlor where heavy curtains shielded windows. Under each bed, into shadowed areas, we searched; her presence loosened the tension knotting my shoulders.

At last she exhaled, straightening. "Done. No sign of him."

I drew her close, inhaling the faint trace of lavender in her hair. "Is that so, Doctor?" I teased, pulling her into my arms.

She squealed, pressing her cheek to my chest just like she had in that damp cave—warmth seeping through my shirt.

Raising the silk tie, I feigned severity. "There's a report of malpractice," I declared, voice softening. "You're under arrest."

Claudia's lower lip quivered. I turned her gently, guiding her hands to the front and then looping her wrists with the tie's supple silk. Before she could object, her lips found mine—urgent, sweet. My hands roamed the curve of her waist, fingertips grazing the smoothness of her body. The rest of the world fell away.

I led her along the hallway by memory, each kiss stoking a fire beneath my ribs. In her room, moonlight spilled over rumpled sheets. I laid her down and captured her hands above her head, letting my lips trail kisses along her throat to the slope of her collarbone. Her fingers tangled in my hair, tugging me closer. I lifted her hands again.

Unlacing her dress was a delicious challenge: silk threads slipping from my slick fingers as my mouth worshipped her skin. At last, the fabric was away from her body, and I freed myself of my own clothes, the cool air heightening every nerve ending. I pressed my lips to the gentle swell of her breast, tracing the edge with my tongue until her breath hitched.

Gliding lower, I brushed my lips against the inside of her thigh, tasting the salt of her skin. She exhaled sharply. When my tongue met her clit, a moan tumbled from her. Gently at first, then insistent, my finger joined the dance, each movement drawing her body into smooth waves of pleasure until she shuddered and cried out my name.

I pulled up, lips damp and eager, and positioned myself above her. Her hands clenched in my hair as I slid in, slow at first, feeling the soft warmth envelop me. With each stroke, her hips lifted, matching my rhythm. The mattress creaked under us; the scent of our breaths mingled in the hush.

I picked up the pace with growing urgency, each pulse a summons to release. She arched beneath me, voice rising in breathless gasps. I held her close, whispering her name as we surged together into a frenzied peak. The moment cracked open—a burst of light and heat—binding us in a shared pulse of bliss.

We collapsed, limbs entwined, hearts hammering in unison. The moonlight filtered through the curtains as we drifted into a soft, sated sleep, still wrapped in the afterglow of our intimacy.

"Alex, can you hear me?" Claudia's voice drifted through a haze of rose-tinted shadows, and for a moment I thought I'd slid into some sweet afterlife where she waited for me. Her fingers cradled my jaw, gentle as moth wings, and she placed kiss after kiss along my cheek and lips. Just as I reached up to pull her closer, the heavy weight of a quilt shifted around me with a soft rustle. This wasn't heaven. My eyes fluttered open to pale morning light filtering through pink curtains. The warm glow revealed an Art Deco dream: black lacquered end tables with chrome inlays, a scalloped headboard of cream leather, and gilded frames holding stylized portraits of women in flapper dresses.

"Thank God, you're awake," Claudia said, her white silk robe slipping off one shoulder. She had pinned her dark hair back with a mother-of-pearl comb, and her smile shone brighter than the sunrise. "I thought you'd sleep the day away."

"And miss a moment with you?" I croaked, voice crackling like an old radio. "Never. I must just be tired from our travels and my healing."

Claudia scooted closer, her knee brushing mine and sending a warm jolt through my thigh. "Let me see." She parted the fabric and laid both palms flat against my side, her touch like sunlight seeping into cold stone. "You appear to be healthy."

My throat tightened. "How long was I out?"

She reached for a tall glass of water on the bedside table, the condensation beading on its surface. With one hand she tipped my chin up, and I drank, tasting only the clean, chilling slide of water down my throat. When she set the glass back, I pressed my palm to her forearm. "I think I can sit up, Doctor."

She propped pillows behind my back. "I have to look after my patients," she said with a smile. Then, her forehead rested against mine, and I felt the faint heartbeat of her emotions, pulsing through skin to skin.

"I have a very good doctor indeed." I brushed a thumb along her cheekbone and leaned in for a kiss. Her lips were soft and warm; my heart thundered so loud I thought she'd hear it in my chest. She deepened the kiss, then gently drew my bottom lip between hers and tugged just enough to make me ache for more. A rush of need flooded me—I'd never wanted anything more than I wanted her in that moment. If Marie finally ended those dual timelines, we'd have years—decades, lifetimes—to make up for every second apart.

Claudia broke away, mock concern flickering across her dark eyes. "Are you sure you're fully healthy?"

I pressed my lips to her collarbone, where her robe fell open. "How will I ever repay you for your services?" My fingers curved around the swell of her breast beneath the silk, and her skin warmed to a delicate blush.

She shifted back, giving me space. "We still need to be certain Marie stops the timelines."

I nodded, heart still pounding. "Absolutely."

"Good thing everyone will be here soon," she said with a playful smirk, sliding my pajama top off my shoulders as I reluctantly swung my legs over the side of the bed.

I slipped on my shirt and pants while she put on a dress and brushed a loose curl from her temple. I could watch her take off a robe every day for the rest of my life. The staircase below creaked under my feet as we descended. The hallway light pooled in pale rectangles on the carpet patterned with tulip motifs, and I followed Claudia into a bright living room where voices tangled like well-worn threads.

"I'm worried about Marie," Nelly said, her hands twisting in the loose sleeves of her sweater.

"Claudia managed to glimpse the situation," Olinda replied calmly, arms folded as she peered at a shelf of books.

Florian waved a hand at the mix of bold prints and antique wood around her. "Oh, how I love this décor—Claudia's mother has such taste."

"It's pretty snazzy," Frank agreed, tossing a red-leafed maple branch into a tall vase.

"I'll make lunch," Kiersten announced and headed for the kitchen archway. "Who wants to help?"

"I will," Thomas said, rolling up his sleeves and striding after her.

"Claudia's right," Lina added, padding over to a low bookshelf. Her fingers danced across rows of leather-bound volumes. "Her mother left some truly helpful tomes."

"Wow, these are amazing," James murmured, lifting a heavy folio with reverent care.

"They won't help with what we need now," Anna said, stepping forward. Her eyes were sharp. Claudia and I exchanged glances as Anna's voice grew firmer. "You had the sight back in Ireland, correct?"

Claudia's breath caught. "Ye—yes," she whispered, staring at Anna.

"And it worked on anyone who hadn't already reincarnated?"

Another nod. Sweat beaded on Claudia's temples.

"When you returned, it had vanished," Anna declared, her voice a whisper of urgency, as Claudia nodded in agreement. "But now it's returned, sparing only those who have not reincarnated."

The room was filled with eyes watching Claudia's chorus of nods. I recalled how she had effortlessly read my earlier thoughts.

"So, by touching me, you should be able to witness my past life as it shifts, with Elizabeth alongside Marie," Anna concluded with an air of finality.

"Did you know this would happen to your sight?" I demanded, my eyes boring into Claudia. "And didn't tell me before you touched me?"

She didn't need to respond. The truth crashed over me like a tidal wave. We had no secrets now. "Clau-di-a!" I cried, the name a desperate plea in the suffocating silence.

"I love you," she said through a smirk.

"I love you to…" My decree was silenced with her kiss.

CHAPTER NINETEEN – MARIE

Walking to Mary's cottage through the mist-shrouded lanes, I contemplate how to convince her weathered hands to weave the spell that would reincarnate Elizabeth, herself, and Barnabus. The cries of battle—hoarse, desperate, and triumphant—surround me like invisible specters. The cobblestoned main street appears ahead, but soldiers in mud-splattered uniforms swarm like angry wasps, their steel glinting dully in the gray light.

I duck into a narrow lane with crumbling stone walls, its emptiness a blessing. Fifty yards ahead, a cluster of ancient oak trees offers better cover. You'd think soldiers wouldn't attack a civilian, but I remember the haunted eyes of victims after Cromwell's men finished their bloody work the first time. An enemy party suddenly bursts from the street into my sanctuary, their boots thundering against the packed earth. They barrel toward me—faces contorted with fear—and I press myself against the nearest building, rough stone scraping my back through my dress.

They sprint past, reeking of sweat and gunpowder, and a battalion of Irishmen with wild eyes and fierce expressions chase after them, their weapons raised high. Well, that's different from before. I straighten my spine and wait until the coast is completely clear, my heart still hammering against my ribs. The ringing crash and bang of swords—metal on metal—

echoes around the corner where the men are now engaged in their deadly dance. I whisper a prayer that the men from Drogheda, with their familiar accents and faces, will emerge victorious.

I retrace my steps, boots splashing through puddles, to find a different path. Jogging through the street with my skirts bunched in my fists, I spy an empty alley between two sagging buildings and slip into its shadows. As I make my way along the damp passage, a cloaked shadow materializes at the far end, moving with a familiar gait. My first instinct is to turn back, but the sounds of fighting—grunts and screams—echo from that direction. It's only one shadow, slight and feminine, so I continue forward, one hand reaching for the small knife hidden in my bodice.

"Laura?" the shadow asks in a voice like dried leaves, and I recognize its raspy timbre immediately.

"Elizabeth, what are you doing out here?" I ask, taking in her pallid face and the dark circles beneath her once-bright eyes.

She tries to answer me, but a coughing fit racks her frail body, bending her double as she covers her mouth with a handkerchief already spotted with crimson.

"Have you taken the medicine I gave you?" I ask, steadying her trembling shoulders.

She nods an affirmative, her hair limp against her damp forehead, and when she can finally speak again, her voice is threadbare. "I was heading to Mary's to see if her herbs and incantations can heal what ails my lungs. The medicine helped dull the pain but wasn't enough to stop the blood."

I put my arm through hers, feeling the bones beneath her sleeve like a bird's, supporting her as we walk to Mary's house with its smoke-darkened thatch. "Why did you help me back at the tent?" I ask, studying her profile.

"Lochlainn and I are trying to keep the casualties to a minimum in this godforsaken conflict," she whispers, her breath visible in the cool air.

"And who is Lochlainn, really? What binds him to this cause?" I press.

"You met him in my husband's tent—the tall one with the scar across his jaw."

"I know his face, but why is he in this with you? What does he gain?"

"Because I recruited him," she says with a ghost of her old smile.

I'm not sure how to respond to that revelation, but more protection for my sister doesn't sound like a bad thing to me in these dangerous times. Elizabeth must notice my look of bewilderment, my brow furrowed like freshly plowed fields, because she continues with a gentle squeeze of my arm.

Elizabeth's dark hair falls in soft waves over her shoulders as she leans forward, eyes glittering with something urgent.

"Well, not exactly 'recruit'. You know those two men who trail Oliver like living shadows?"

I press my lips together, the late-afternoon sun slicing through the mist. My mind flicks to the figures I'd glimpsed at Oliver's side. "Yes," I murmur, heart fluttering with curiosity. "They're the counters—but I always assumed Lochlainn was one of them, too. Wait... You made a counter?"

She presses a finger to my lips before I can shout. Her touch is cool; a hush falls over us. "When I died during the Prohibition timeline, all my memories from every timeline flooded back. I remember every one of them now."

My pulse hammers in my ears. "But I've always carried memories from other timelines once reincarnation began," I say, recalling why Mary didn't yet. I meet her gaze. "Your reincarnation hasn't happened?"

Elizabeth closes her eyes, as if revisiting a distant storm. "Apparently, when Oliver spun off those counter timelines, dozens of your diaries showed up in every timeline. My theory is that the lives you wrote about somehow latched onto them."

I frown. "That sounds more like a hypothesis than a solid theory," I challenge softly. "Either that or Oliver's dual timelines are warping reality more than we realized. So... you learned about all this because of my diaries?"

She clasps and then unclasps her hands, each movement deliberate. "Not one entry in particular, but they led me to discover reincarnation. Which is how I persuaded Mary to reincarnate me—and our lost child."

A cold hush settles in my chest. "I see," I whisper, brushing a hand through my hair. "I'm relieved you got that chance—but the upheaval from your husband's meddling worries me."

Elizabeth's brow furrows; agitation ripples beneath her skin. She begins to pace, brushing her ankles against her dress. "Then why else would I need my own counter?" she demands.

I watch her, voice small. "I'm still trying to sort it out."

She halts, locking eyes with me. "About what?"

I swallow, heart pounding. "If Oliver's magic is so potent, did he simply merge his future soul into his past body—two souls sharing one flesh—so he wouldn't have to time travel?"

A bitter smile tugs at her lips. She folds her arms, shadowed by hazy sunlight. "Time travel is beyond his skill. Once he caught wind of your plans, he improvised. He didn't have much choice."

My brow lifts. "Why was he so upset about me saving you?"

She sweeps her hands to her cheeks, exasperation softening into triumph. "He knew that if you succeeded, you'd cut his reincarnation cycle. But the joke's on him—"

"Jokes on him?" I echo, confusion twisting my stomach.

"By fusing two souls into one body," she says, voice steady, "he inadvertently ended his own cycle. No more rebirth."

A wave of relief floods me, immediately shadowed by Elizabeth's sorrow. I reach out, cushioning her elbow. "I'm sorry."

Her gaze snaps to me, mild anger flickering in her eyes. "No, you're not."

My throat tightens. "You can still make the best life with him in this timeline."

Her shoulders straighten, resolve radiating from her posture. "Yes. And now, with him out of the picture, I can keep our child safe across every future timeline."

Moments later, we find ourselves standing on Mary's crooked doorstep, my heart pounding. The wood groans as we step inside. The familiar scent of lavender and old tomes hits me, a swirl of nostalgia and unease.

"Elizabeth, you frightened me," Mary exclaims, smoothing her apron. Concern furrows her brow. "Where have you been?"

A tall figure materializes behind her—Barnabus—arms crossed, gaze sharpening. "And who is this?"

Elizabeth's voice trembles with caution. "This is Laura."

Mary's eyes widen as she studies me, then she takes a careful step forward, curiosity softening her features. "Have we met before?"

"I think I saw you in town," Barnabus says, brushing straw from his coat sleeve as he settles onto a stool beside the hearth.

"She's with Étaín's circle now," Elizabeth answers for me, her voice soft as she peers down at the simmering pot. "Laura just recently arrived."

Mary's gaze swings to me, her forehead creasing. "No—I feel something... connected to you."

Elizabeth's eyes widen so far I fear they'll pop free of their sockets. The firelight dances in her pupils. I can't waste another second. "That's because I'm your soul reborn, sent backward through time."

Mary's knees buckle and she sways; Barnabus slides a chair behind her and steadies her by the elbows. When her breathing steadies, she huffs, "Start at the beginning."

"I will," I promise, but the rasping cough that rips from Elizabeth interrupts me like a guillotine.

Barnabus leans forward. "What's the matter, dear?"

I press a finger to my lips, then whisper, "This is how she died the first time. I brought medicine—well, Claudia gave it to me—but it won't keep the fever at bay."

Mary's eyes fly open. "Claudia?"

"I'll explain." I nod toward Elizabeth, who's rubbing her throat.

Mary straightens, clutching Barnabus's arm to help Elizabeth into the chair by the hearth. "Fetch dandelion leaves from the garden," she commands me. Then, to Barnabus: "Bring goat's milk."

I slip outside, the cold air prickling my cheeks as I bend to rip bright-green leaves from their stems. Inside, Barnabus ladles milk into the blackened kettle while Elizabeth coughs again, clutching her chest. Mary unlocks a cabinet and retrieves a small glass jar of pale-blue healing water.

I turn, basket in hand. Barnabus stirs the milk until it simmers, then I drop in the dandelion leaves. They bubble and soften in a green swirl. Mary watches me, lips curled in encouragement.

When the brew is thick and fragrant, Mary pours it into a wooden bowl and sets it before Elizabeth. Barnabus uncorks the jar and holds it ready. All four of us lean close.

In hushed, measured tones we intone:

"Lady of the flame,

Lady of healing,

Lady of pure love,

Lady Brigid!

On behalf of our sick one,

May she find your healing

Power aflame in her soul.

So mote it be."

Elizabeth sips, first the warm dandelion stew, then the cool, minty water. I watch her features soften: the deep hollows under her eyes fill in, her cheeks flush rose-pink, and the haze in her gaze lifts. Mary drapes an arm around her shoulders, pressing her face to Elizabeth's hair.

Mary turns to me, voice trembling with awe. "Tell me, how do you know Claudia?"

I swallow, meeting her hopeful gaze. "Claudia is my daughter." I hesitate, then add, "Or—your daughter, reborn."

Barnabus goes pale. "You mean our daughter walked these woods, and we never knew?"

I nod. "Unless you two find your way into the next life again, Claudia will never be born."

They exchange startled looks, voices tumbling over each other in quiet panic and wonder. At last, Barnabus turns back to me. "So—across every timeline, we remain a family?"

"For the most part," I say, giving Mary's hand a gentle squeeze.

Mary's eyes fill with tears of relief. "With our child."

I trace the flicker of flame in the hearth, feeling a strange ache as though looking into her very soul. "I came back to save Elizabeth," I explain softly. "Her husband meddled with fate— wove chaos into the strands of time and nearly destroyed everything."

"That sounds about right," Mary says, nodding with the certainty of someone who knew all along. She turns to her sister with a triumphant look. "I told you," she adds, a hint of satisfaction in her voice.

After a tense discussion, they finally agree to reincarnate themselves, a decision that feels like a heavy weight lifting off my chest. I can breathe again. We gather in a tight circle for a group hug, feeling the warmth of shared determination. Quickly, we gather essentials, preparing to slip away from the chaos of battle through the gate. The narrow alleys, shadowed and twisting, have become second nature to us as we dart from one to another.

There are two Northern gates, but the one we initially aimed for is heavily guarded, forcing us to opt for the second and plan to loop back. Lochlainn waits for us just outside the gate, his eyes scanning the area with vigilant precision.

Elizabeth halts abruptly outside the gate we originally intended to use. Her eyes narrow as she looks around with an unsettled expression. "I do sense something off now, but it has nothing to do with you seeing each other," she says, her voice laced with concern.

"What is it?" I ask, anxiety creeping into my voice.

"Reincarnating my lost child before the curse was broken means the curse will carry on!" Elizabeth exclaims, her words hanging heavily in the air.

A cacophony of clashing swords and shouting erupts on the other side of the gate, the sound of battle rising like a storm. I tighten my grip on Elizabeth's arm. "We'll discuss how to handle that at the cave where it's safe," I assure her, urgency threading through my words.

An arrow slices through the air, mere inches past Mary's head. Barnabus immediately wraps his arm around her, pulling her close and acting as a human shield. Without another word, we sprint away from the danger, driven by the instinct to survive.

CHAPTER TWENTY – CROMWELL

"May you leave without returning,

May you fall without rising,

May the cat eat you, and the devil eat the cat."

(An Irish Curse)

Oliver's mount thundered across churned earth, sweat and dust rising in its wake. With a fierce cry, he bore down on the enemy line, steel ringing as his sword arced through the air. It bit into flesh again and again, each strike sending hot blood spraying like crimson fireworks against the sky. All around him, horses neighed, and men screamed, but when he glanced over his shoulder, the shouts behind him belonged only to his own men—no reinforcements had come.

In an instant, a dark shape loomed at his side: another rider's lance found his saddle-flank, unseating him. He hit the ground with a gasp, the world tilting beneath him. As he fought to rise, his eyes fixed on the ramparts: Marie/Laura, Barnabus, Mary, and his wife, lined like statues in the light. Then Lochlainn stepped forward. Why did he stand idle? Rage ignited in Oliver's chest, a wildfire stoked by betrayal.

Driven by fury, Oliver rolled to his knees and sprang up, sword whirling in a lethal dance. He stabbed and slashed, each blow sending a ripple of retreat through the foe. They parted, opening a narrow corridor toward his scattered soldiers. Hope flared—but before he could reach it, a searing pain ripped through his thigh. He staggered, the world spinning as he collapsed onto the blood-soaked ground.

A mounted Irish cavalryman reined in close, blade raised in one slow, deliberate arc. The steel found its mark at Oliver's throat, shearing through collar and chest in a gout of warmth. Stars exploded behind his lids; the agony was a living inferno that refused to let him go. He sank toward unconsciousness, every breath a knife, but clung to one prayer: that Ruarc and Aodhán would somehow find him.

As darkness encroached, a vision shimmered into being: a carnival of shadows in a Kansas City haunted house, lights flickering over his lost boy's face, framed by a short, sobering beard. "Dad," the child whispered—then a cable snapped with a scream of metal, and a counterweight crushed him in an instant. Oliver's heart fractured all over again. Why did death claim his children so cruelly?

Memories surged: Elizabeth's ritual to reincarnate their child, the curse she had too late broken, Mary's part in weaving fate's threads—each decision echoing across centuries. He realized now: he must reach Elizabeth, unlock the secret of time's river, and force her to break the curse before Mary's hand could shape their destiny. Revenge or salvation—he would have both.

But the world was darkening. Blood pooled beneath him, warmth ebbing fast. No cavalry thundered to his side. From the battlements came the triumphant roar of "Drogheda abú!"—a chorus that proclaimed his siege a ruin. The thought of capture, a living trophy for the enemy, tightened his chest more than any blade. As the battlefield's noise faded, Oliver Cromwell lay still, clutching his dying purpose in the gathering gloom.

The next vision slammed into Oliver's consciousness like a freight train, more vivid than the last. At his gleaming research facility nestled in the distant future, Oliver had lost his beloved wife and cherubic son to monstrous alien vultures with razor-sharp beaks and wingspans that blotted out the sun. The young boy in his vision—rosy-cheeked with unruly brown curls—was from the golden days before the vulture attack. He'd bounce through the sterile white corridors, his laughter echoing off the walls, making even the most serious scientists crack smiles with his elaborate make-believe worlds and impromptu games of tag.

He'd transformed Oliver's tedious days into adventures filled with wonder and joy. When his wife's melodic voice and his child's infectious giggles were silenced forever, the facility's bright fluorescent lights seemed dimmer, the white walls grayer, as if a permanent shadow had fallen over everything. Now, standing before him in blood-soaked clothes, his son's translucent form asked, "Daddy, do you want to play a game?" His voice echoed as if coming from the bottom of a well.

"Of course," Oliver croaked through his parched throat.

"Guess what I'm thinking?" The boy's eyes were unnaturally bright, almost glowing.

"I don't know," Oliver gurgled, tasting copper as warm blood bubbled between his lips. "Tell me."

"You shouldn't have brought two souls into one body." The words hung in the air like icicles.

"What do you mean?" Oliver asked, but the boy dissolved like mist in morning sunlight.

The world twisted and warped as another vision assaulted his senses. A couple decades before the Prohibition Era's speakeasies and jazz clubs, he'd been in a polished mahogany carriage with brass fittings when something, maybe a snake, had spooked the chestnut horses. They'd reared up, nostrils flaring, before bolting down the street. The carriage had overturned, wood splintering like gunshots. Anna her belly swollen with promise beneath her lace-trimmed dress, had suffered a miscarriage, her tears soaking the silk pillowcase for weeks afterward.

Now he saw the teenager who might have been—tall and lanky with Anna's piercing eyes and his own cleft chin. They were playing catch in their sun-dappled backyard, the leather baseball making a satisfying smack as it landed in well-worn gloves. Golden light filtered through maple leaves, casting dancing shadows on the freshly cut grass. It was a glorious day, the air sweet with the scent of nearby lilacs, and Oliver felt as if everything in the universe had aligned perfectly. Then the child fixed him with those familiar eyes and said, "Now you won't be able to reincarnate." His voice carried the weight of ancient wisdom.

"What do you mean?" Oliver sputtered, a cold dread seeping into his bones.

"Two souls in one body doesn't allow that," said his sweet child, twirling the baseball in long, elegant fingers. "But don't worry. Mom will reincarnate so she'll be with me." His smile was both beautiful and terrible.

As the vision dissolved like watercolors in rain, desperation flooded Oliver's every cell. Was it true? What cruel fate had he unwittingly crafted for himself? What was he going to do?

He felt rough hands upon his clammy skin. The medics had arrived in their blood-spattered uniforms, their faces grim beneath sweat-soaked brows. They applied pressure to his gaping wound after inspecting it with probing fingers and giving rapid-fire orders in Irish, their accents thick as fog. He couldn't understand their harsh, clipped words. They were probably going to lock him in a dank cell after they patched him together with crude stitches. It was like a sick joke played by a malevolent god.

He should have been successful and taken Drogheda, its ancient stone walls now forever beyond his reach. Putting two souls in one body had been done to make sure Marie—with her knowing eyes and interfering ways—didn't meddle in his plans, just like the counters had been created to set her back in their cosmic game. It had all been so that he could be with his family, to feel his wife's soft breath against his neck at night and his son's small hand in his once more. Had he gotten a little overzealous in his selfish desire for power? Sure, but who doesn't crave just a little more than they deserve?

Once the medics slid him onto a tent bed beneath the flickering lantern light, the acrid scent of blood and alcohol stung Oliver's nostrils. His head throbbed in time with distant moans. Through the rough canvas walls of the makeshift field hospital, he caught ragged English voices.

"We'll never take Ireland now," murmured a man whose uniform was spattered with mud and crimson—one of Oliver's own, grievously wounded beside him.

"Now the Irish will build more ships and join Spain and France against us," another added, voice low, spitting curses.

"I bet the country reverts to Brehon Law and abandons Christianity altogether," the first soldier sneered.

Oliver forced his jaw to lock, every word a blow. "Don't be fools," he barked. Pain lanced through his ribs, but he straightened in the cot. "We've lost the battle, not the war. We'll regroup and take Wexford. How dare you surrender your spirit so easily."

The first man sat up shakily, palm raised as though to lift an invisible helmet. His arm hovered awkwardly in empty air.

"Help me to my feet," Oliver ordered, swinging his legs over the side. He smelled sweat and desperation. "Is the coast clear? It feels like night, but I've lost all sense of time."

"There'll be another round of medics in twenty minutes, then they'll withdraw to sleep," the second man offered, fear trembling in his tone.

"We'll slip away once they're out cold," Oliver replied, voice hoarse. "How many of our ships remain?"

"They've already sailed off, Sir—safer to risk the sea than to be taken here," the first man said. "That was three days gone."

Oliver's heart clenched. "And Ruarc? Aodhán?"

"No sign of them, Sir," came the hollow answer.

Silence fell heavy until the next team of medics bustled in. One knelt to peel back Oliver's bloodstained bandages. The odor of festering flesh made him wince. The medic exhaled, shaking his head.

"What is it?" Oliver rasped.

"The infection's deepened," the man said flatly. "If you wish, I can fetch quill and parchment for your final requests."

Oliver's hand shot out, gripping the medic's collar. "How dare you!" His voice cracked. "I'm—going—to be fine!"

The medic slid free and stepped back. "Suit yourself." He left, closing the tent flap with a soft clap.

As the last lantern guttered, Oliver drifted into fevered visions. He saw Claudia and Alex, their laughter echoing through sunlit halls—mocking him. Then Marie, surrounded by thriving villagers, guiding them with gentle smiles, her community basking in knowledge and abundance. Guilt and rage churned his gut, but what followed froze his blood.

He stood in brilliant midday light beside Elizabeth, whom he loved, and in the crowd's awe, Lochlainn kissed her as if they'd just wed. Oliver's own children—bright-faced, trusting—rushed to embrace Lochlainn in joyous abandon. Fury, hotter than any fever, boiled beneath his skin. He woke drenched in sweat: sheets clinging, hair plastered to his forehead. Around him, his men lay still, surrendered to sleep rather than flight.

Summoning what strength remained, he eased himself from the cot and crept through the canvas flaps into the damp night. He staggered, crumpling into the dew-soaked grass, eyes fixed on the pale moon's silver glow. Drawing breath ragged with pain and purpose, he whispered an ancient incantation:

"I banish you left

I banish you right

I banish you now

Out of sight.

I send you, I send you,

To the counter world

I have wrought.

No longer shall you

Interfere with my

Timelines."

With each line, wind whipped the grass, and the moonlight danced unnaturally across his pale skin. In that moment, the souls of Mary, Barnabus, Claudia, Alex—and even Elizabeth, with all their kin—were hurled into the shadowed counter world he commanded. He roared triumphantly, but a violent shudder wracked his body as the infection ignited every artery, every nerve.

From the swirling darkness at his feet came a small voice, trembling: "Father… don't you see what you've done?" A child emerged, eyes bright with sorrow.

Oliver reached out, voice soft. "Come here, sweet child. Let me tell you a story."

The boy drifted closer, a single tear tracking down dusty cheeks. Oliver recited the bedtime tale he once told his children in the 17th century—of a cunning cat whose cleverness raised his master to greatness. As the final words fell, the child's face twisted in heartbreak rather than delight.

"What's wrong?" Oliver whispered, pressing a trembling hand to the boy's face.

"You banished me too!" the child sobbed. "Now I'm bound to that counter world forever!"

In a gust of wind, the boy vanished, carried away into the unseen realm. Oliver's vision blurred. The moon was snuffed out, plunging him into pitch black. With one final, rattling breath, he sank into the cold earth. Oliver Cromwell was gone, never to rise again.

Guarded Time

CHAPTER TWENTY-ONE - CLAUDIA

"May your thoughts be as glad as the shamrocks.

May your heart be as light as a song.

May each day bring you bright, happy hours

That stay with you all the year long."

(An Irish Blessing)

As my fingertips brush Anna's arm, the flicker of torchlight reveals Mother kneeling beside Elizabeth, Lochlainn, Mary, and Barnabus. They're in our cavern, the damp stone walls echoing their whispered incantations. Each syllable shivers through the stale air, weaving around Elizabeth's slight form as they strive to break the Cromwell curse that clings to her child's soul. I clear my throat. "They're all right," I whisper, and a soft murmur of relief ripples through our circle.

Nelly's eyes sparkle with determination. "Can we speak to them... or pull Marie back here?" Her question hangs in the air, as weighty as the huge fountain in the ballroom.

Olinda nods, her hair catching the light from the chandelier. "Excellent idea."

Anna tilts her head in confusion. "Which is it—talking or extracting?"

Nelly grins, that playful twist of her lips returning. "Let's at least warn Marie before we terrify her stiff." There's laughter in her voice, a spark against the air's chill.

I exhale slowly. "The hawthorn tree behind the house— that's where Mother chose to thin the veil." My voice is hushed with realization. Memories of our trip to Drogheda flood in: the wind-swept moor, the trees bowing under ancient secrets. Alex's smile is soft, and heat blooms in my chest.

Anna's eyes brighten. "Perfect. The hawthorn is folklore's threshold to the faerie realm."

Kiersten volunteers cheerfully, "I can pack up lunch for a picnic." We emerge from the house into a world filtered by golden late morning light.

We spread a quilt beneath the fluttering boughs of the hawthorn. The bark is knobbly, pale blossoms brushing our hair as they drift down. Everyone tucks into crusty bread, cheese, and thick apple tart—though my stomach twists in anxiety. Olinda offers crackers; I shake my head, pressing a hand to my belly. After we've eaten, Alex arranges a handful of rose petals, wild strawberries, and a sprig of thyme as our offering. Together we raise our voices:

"I will pull the moon,

The herb blessing by the Earth;

So long as I preserve,

No distance shall contain,

And I will speak to them."

A hush falls. The breeze shifts, stirring the leaves into a whispering chorus.

At first, I see Marie's stunned face appear—pale, wide-eyed against a backdrop of torchlight. I call, "Mother!" But static crackles like distant thunder, leaves spiral into a vortex around us, and suddenly the ground dips away. We all rise from the quilt—our bodies and those in 1649—hovering as though buoyed by unseen currents. My lungs seize with that disorienting rush I felt the first time I tumbled through time. A cold dread coils in my gut: something darker underpins this passage.

When the spinning world steadies, I find Alex's hands cupping my cheeks, checking me with fierce concern. "You're all right?" His voice trembles. Around me, Frank rubs at his ears; Thomas peers into the distance.

A voice cries, "Claudia?" in Mother's familiar cadence. We're all here—everyone from both centuries.

Lina breaks the stunned hush. "That's the lighthouse we spotted from the ship." She points, and sure enough, a stone tower stands on a rocky promontory, a bonfire blazing at its base—just as we'd seen aboard the S.S. Hewitt. Nothing about this makes sense.

"How did we end up here?" I whisper.

Anna's eyes flash. "A final curse from Oliver, no doubt."

Alex grips my hand. "Can you send us home?"

Anna shrugs, as calm as if discussing the weather. "No battles to fight now that Cromwell's gone." I glance at her, uneasy: how does she know he's truly dead?

James adjusts his coat. "We've time-traveled," he announces, voice equal parts wonder and excitement. Florian pumps her fist. Nelly rushes forward to embrace Marie, whose tears shine in the firelight.

"Introduce us," Olinda urges, voice warm. "Or at the reception."

"Reception?" I echo, breath catching.

Olinda lays a hand gently on my abdomen. "You two are overdue for a proper wedding, especially with a baby on the way." Her raised brow is teasing, insistent.

Alex's grin lights every shadow; a rose flushes my cheeks. He pauses, eyes softening. "We're going to be parents?" His question trembles with hope. When I nod, he sweeps me into his arms, and I can feel my heart pounding in reply.

Mary and Barnabus step forward, each placing a hand on our shoulders—Mary on mine, Barnabus on Alex's. Elizabeth and Lochlainn approach, kindness in their eyes; Kiersten and Florian clasp hands in joyful solidarity. Frank, Thomas, and James toss their hats skyward, the echoes of cheers scattering over the rugged shoreline. Alex suddenly kneels, pulling a simple silver ring from his pocket. "Claudia," he says, voice thick with emotion, "would you do me the extraordinary honor of becoming my wife?"

Time stills; the salt wind drifts through my hair, brimming with promise. A tremor of doubt knits his brows—until I answer, "Yes."

He lifts me effortlessly, spins me around. His thumbs brush beneath my jaw, his gaze melts from my eyes to my lips. I lean in, and our kiss is gentle fire—careful, reverent, despite the crowd around us. Foreheads pressed together, we smile, breath mingling in the moonlight. In this other world—this other time—I feel a tether of love stronger than any spell or curse.

Here, with my family and friends gathered, I know that imperfection can be beautiful. My heart swells at the knowledge I have everything I ever wanted.

THE END

ACKNOWLEDGMENTS

Guarded Time exists today because of an incredible network of support and collaboration. I am filled with immense gratitude, even though words cannot fully express it. Nonetheless, I will attempt to convey my appreciation here.

A huge thank you to the brilliant minds who shared their creativity and organization skills, and supported this book's journey in countless ways: Kelly Allenby, James Young, Caroline Trussell, and Amy Brewer. Their ideas, inspiration, and advice have been invaluable.

I am also grateful to the communities and medical teams who have guided me through my journey with deafness. About a year before writing *Armored Hours*, I experienced a ruptured eardrum in my non-deaf ear. During treatment, a cyst was discovered in my brain. Six months before the pre-order went live, another cyst was found but the first one had shrunk. With your ongoing guidance and support, we continue in search of answers.

Lastly, thank you to my children for their unwavering belief in me and their limitless love. When I write about a mother's love, I draw from the beautiful experience of being your mother. I am fortunate to have such awesome children like you in my life.

THANK YOU FOR READING

Did you enjoy this book?

We invite you to leave a review on the website of your choice.

DID YOU KNOW THAT LEAVING A REVIEW…

- Helps other readers find books

- Allows your voice to be heard

- Gives author recognition for their work

- Doesn't have to be long. A couple likes is perfect

DON'T MISS YOUR NEXT FAVORITE BOOK

https://hypothesis-productions.yolasite.com/

ABOUT THE AUTHOR

Stephanie Hansen is a PenCraft and Global Book Award Winning Author as well as an Imadjinn finalist. Her debut novella series, *Altered Helix*, released in 2020. It hit the #1 New Release, #1 Best Seller, and other top 100 lists on Amazon. It is now being adapted to an animated story for Tales. Her debut novel, *Replaced Parts*, released in 2021 through Fire & Ice YA and Tantor Audio. It has been in a Forbes article, hit Amazon bestseller lists, and made the Apple young adult coming soon bestsellers list. The second book in the *Transformed Nexus* series, *Omitted Pieces*, releases in 2022. Her debut spicy paranormal romance, Ghostly Howls, released 2023. Armored Hours released 2024. She is a member of the deaf and hard of hearing community, so she tries to incorporate that into her fiction. https://www.authorstephaniehansen.com/

DON'T MISS MORE FROM THE EPIC ENCHANTED TRAVELERS UNIVERSE

https://www.amazon.com/dp/B0FSXRJLYY/